Everything and Nothing

Emma Jordan

Everything and Nothing Copyright © 2020 by Emma Jordan

For Eve, still always my favourite reader and writer.

1
Elle

Late August

My sister is going to kill me.

I'm already an hour late to the launch party of Lucy and Cain's new writing retreat, Nashville Narrators, but there is absolutely nothing to wear in either of Lucy's wardrobes. I can't very well turn up in a silk robe, either. This isn't Boston.

No party started until I was there anyway.

I shove the clothes to one side, again, in order to find something to wear to go shopping for a new dress. The outfits I'd brought definitely favoured the night, but sparkle and glitter just didn't seem right for a lunch – maybe dinner by the time I actually arrived – party in the middle of nowhere, Tennessee.

The only night life here actually hoots or chirps or pretends to be an amphibious bassist.

I rummage in the back of the wardrobe – even after three years living in the States I still keep my outfits in the very European device. A closet seems such a vast space. I just wish I'd maybe thought a little more about my outfit choices during packing. But, I'd expected to be able to shop whilst I hung out with everyone over the summer.

I was fed up to my hind teeth of cowgirl boots and gingham. I missed Boston more than I realised. Oh, for a work-out in the Copley Place mall.

'Come in! Will just be two seconds!' I yell to a knock on the door, as I grab a black pantsuit from a Bloomingdale's box and turn around.

'Jam!' I holler, wrapping my robe around me, as Cain's drummer leans lazily against the doorframe, long brown hair nestled on honeyed brown forearms.

'Lucy is wearing a hole out in the floor downstairs. I thought I'd see where you were.'

Why have I never paid much attention to his eyes, before? Maybe because this is the first time I've been partially dressed before him?

'Clearly here,' I snap. 'Go on; I'll have a champagne waiting for me.'

When he leaves, eventually, I lean back against the opposite wall. That man is almost the right kind of distracting. I'd forgotten what strong upper arm muscles he had, from all the drumming and the surfing.

I shake my head free of such dangerous thoughts and climb into the black jersey suit I'd found, marvelling at the halter neck and very flattering design. This was far too modern for my sister. She probably wouldn't miss it if it came back to Boston with me. I slipped on my favourite zebra print heels, did a final retouch of my hair and make-up in the mirror, satisfied that the trousers at least made the ensemble daytime-suitable.

I was prepared to meet Lucy's wrath.

I made my way through the vast building which Lucy and Cain called their home – each of the eight bedrooms has an en-suite – so far removed from the terraced house in northern England, where we had grown up, or the apartment, a few minutes from Harvard, which had been my home for the last four years. I couldn't wait to own a property like this one day, overlooking the Cape. I'd swap the recording studio basement for a spa, and there would be moored boats, not parked trucks.

'Auntie Elle!' My adorable two year old niece flies into my legs and I scoop her up. She smells gorgeous and chocolately.

'Who's a Chocolate Monster?' I whisper against her shrieks, as she cuddles in to me. 'Where's your Mummy and Daddy?'

'Daddy piano.' Lottie announces, pointing through the house.

'Ah, you captured the escapee.' Jam smiles down at Lottie. I'll carry this across for you.' I turn and Jam stands behind me, a glass of bubbles and a bottle of beer, one in each hand. I nod and walk through to the house to the writing retreat opposite.

I slow my approach as I hear Cain playing a familiar ballad, which I believe had paid for a wing of their home. His playing is simply beautiful. He can turn his hand to any instrument and make it sound incredible. My sister is such a lucky woman.

Lottie wriggles out of my hands and runs towards the door. I follow, and Lucy looks up at our arrival, a perfect smile on her face. Guests stand around the ridiculously happy couple, or sit on sumptuous sofas and equally comfortable chairs. This room is the main feature in the retreat. A huge dining table, big enough for twelve people, takes up one side of the room, but it still seems small in the vast space.

I scan the hundred or so people gathered, as Jam hands me my champagne flute. I interrogate the heads looking in my direction, but immediately disregarded anyone in a flannel shirt. I know half of the scruffy guests are worth a fortune based on their platinum album sales, but I'm only here for the next few days and then I'm flying back to Boston to begin work at an art gallery. Suits and Champagne are my cup of tea.

The song finishes and I pound my heels on the floor and clap my thigh as others cheers. Lucy makes her way to me, enveloping me in a warm hug.

'Elle, you look amazing. Isn't this place wonderful?'

'My erudite sister is lost for adjectives?' I joke.

'I know, I know. I'm just so happy. Let me show you around.' She takes my arm and I follow her throughout the two-storey building, which has been twelve months in the making, even though I've already had several grand tours.

The six private rooms are spacious, with individual writing areas and pampering spaces. The balconies overlook the nearby woods. Lucy has done a wonderful job with the themes of classic and contemporary literature, from the UK and the US. There will be great works created here. We complete the tour and enter the open plan shared space again.

7

Cain and Jam are chatting with guests, Lottie holding both of their hands.

'Look at the beauty in this oak', Lucy marvels, stroking the dining table. 'There will always be food available for our guests, and it will always be laden with gorgeous cakes and glowing faces.'

'You and Cain have created something beautiful. I mean, besides Lottie!'

'Do you think so?'

I nod without hesitation.

'You're already booked up until Christmas, aren't you? As an event coordinator, I know that's no mean feat.'

'Thank you so much for helping with promotion.'

'Uploading a few posts was nothing. The calming *hygge* surrounds sold themselves.'

'You really should visit Copenhagen one day, Elle, you would love it.'

'Oh, no, no, the only travelling these feet are destined for is returning to the north east next week.'

'Elle.' My brother-in-law scoops me into a hug, a genuine embrace that still fools me with its unexpectedness. Except for immediate family, I prefer it when people keep their distance unless it is asked for. I'm so glad he is in Lucy's life. His arms rest around Lucy's shoulder and she naturally sinks into his embrace, a move I've seen hundreds of times these past few weeks, but it always tinkles with my heart. They are absolutely perfect for each other.

I finish the rest of my drink and Jam appears, taking the glass out of my hand. Lottie wanders off with her parents. I smile my thanks, catching a sudden scent of an expensive cologne that I know very well.

Well, well, well.

The party lasts well into the evening, and we relocated to the garden.

Lottie lay sleeping across Cain and Lucy. Cain's manager Sarah and her husband Seb - Cain's guitarist - curl up alongside each other in a love seat. There is a good few years between them in age, but she is younger than her years and he is older than his. They have no children and when they had down time, they travel the country in their little turquoise camper van, Old Blue.

Jam sits on one of the patio sofas, next to a brunette I recognise as one of Lucy's former students who has been studying out here. Tallie, I think she's called; I know she transferred from New England to study her PhD out here with Lucy.

A few other guests linger around high tables, listening to a two-piece band play on the stage. Country music, of course. There is no other kind around here.

I sit on a patio sofa near the window, feet tucked under me, a glass of Tennessee bourbon in my hand, my phone in the other, quite content to let the space work around me. I've been on social media most of the evening, sharing photos of this inspiring and creative place, networking with potential clients – writers, Lucy prefers to call them – and, most importantly, arranging dates for my return to normal life in just six short days.

As the photos uploaded I sipped the amber liquid and glance around. Jam is staring at me and I smile, raising my drink. He whispers something to Tallie and makes his way to my sofa.

'Mind if I sit?' He asks. I shake my head and he flops down onto the cushions. Then he reaches an arm over me, for a quilted throw, and spreads it across us.

'Cold?' I ask.

'Aren't you?'

'I'm from Manchester. This is a heat wave.'

He has a wide smile. But altogether too much hair either side of his face, the brown locks easily brushing his forearms again. I never date guys with more hair than me – who needs a fight for the bathroom?

'When do you go back to Boston?'

'Sunday. I promised Lucy I'd be here for the launch, but I have a new job, and civilisation, to return to.'

'You don't think we're civilised?'

'Well, of course, *you're* travelled. But Nashville could do with a few non-boot related stores.'

His laugh vibrates the cushion beneath us and I find myself scrutinising him. He looks different in this light. And my dates rarely fill out their suits quite as well as a musician fills out a vest.

Cain and Lucy disappear with a still-sleeping Lottie and one by one the guests begin to drift away.

'What are you up to now that Cain's on a touring hiatus?' I ask Jam.

'Going to catch up with my Uncle Eddie in San Diego soon, for a few weeks. Then in November I'm heading off to Thailand.'

'Again? You have a girl down there?'

He shook his head. 'Several.'

'Pardon?'

'I teach music in a school when I visit. Your face, Elle.'

'For that you can buy me another free drink.' I hold out my empty glass. After a brief hesitation he stands and mock bows, heading to the bar.

I trace my fingers along the stems and flowers of the pretty pink and green patchwork quilt now across my knee. I didn't have to check the label to know this was home made. Cain's Mum had recently taken to quilting and I suspected it was one of her projects. It is beautiful. Their guest house in England's western Cornwall is filled with countrified American interior designs, no doubt reflecting her pride in a third of her family. I enjoyed chatting with Nancy, it was a shame they couldn't have stayed for the launch. But they'd be back once the Cornish tourist season quietened down.

Jam returned with my drink, and with a huge bag of crisps; chips would always belong with fish on a plate.

'Hmm, good idea.' I delve into the packet for a handful, settling further into the sofa.

'What's your new job?' He asks.

'I, Elle Rawcliffe, will be the PR Executive for the cutest art gallery in Boston, promoting events for artists to attract wealthy clients.'

'Wow. Congratulations. That sounds like a big deal.'

'It is; I fought hard for this position, interning every chance I could, until they realised how essential I was.' Suddenly his fingers reach for a strand of hair and tuck it behind my ear. I sip my drink, the fire numbing my tongue, while I wait for an explanation.

'I miss your pink hair.'

'It was pretty vulgar.'

'It was pretty.' Apparently, that was the direction he was taking.

'As soon as I stopped dyeing my hair I was taken more seriously. I intend to own my own gallery before I'm twenty-five.'

'That's ... ambitious.'

'The world doesn't hang around.'

He shakes his head.

I reached for his chin with my face, turn him to me, and bring our lips close. For a brief moment I fall into his scent. Then he pulls away, a slight smirk on his face.

'No, Elle. This isn't right.'

'What?'

'You're leaving soon. So am I.'

'Exactly. Think of the possibilities.'

'Elle.'

'Jam.' I reached around for his neck, intending to pull him the short distance to me.

But he is resolute.

I sit up.

Am I being rejected?

As Jam stands, his hands in his pockets, head hung low, I realised I am.

I haven't ever been rejected by a man.

Well, he certainly wasn't worth any further attention.

I rise and stroll into the house, sweeping my hair over my shoulder, knowing my purposeful stride always has an effect on anyone watching.

When I glance over my shoulder, he is in conversation with a musician.

I couldn't believe it.

For the next few days I dive into being fun Auntie Elle, giving Lucy and Cain some much needed time together, before their new venture takes on the life of its own that it is destined to do.

On the last night we were seated around the modest six-seater table in their own dining room, just wrapping up the key lime pie.

'I can't believe you made that, Sis. You only ever operated a microwave.'

She smiles and strokes her daughter's hair.

'I'd still rather read than cook, but this is my absolute favourite American dessert, so I made sure I can make it well. For when the cravings strike again.'

'Be careful how you throw that word around.' I begin. Then catch their expression.

'Oh my absolute world. You're pregnant again?'

Lucy nodded, patting her stomach. 'The baby's due early spring.'

I rushed over to hug my darling sister and then Cain, congratulating them.

The next time I visited I'd be an Aunt twice over. I didn't look anywhere near old enough.

Cain drove me to the airport the next morning, for my ridiculous o'clock flight. We chatted about the lack of glitz in Tennessee and he just laughed. Then I casually asked about Jam, who'd been absent for the last few days.

'Oh, he flew out to San Diego earlier than planned.'

'Oh.' To my recollection I had never caused a man to fly across the country to avoid me.

His loss.

2
Jam

Elle had changed considerably in the years that she'd been studying.

The effervescent, pink-haired, screwball woman had morphed into a corporate, dynamite, raven-haired woman I would do well to avoid.

We had nothing in common. We were almost related by marriage, actually, such was my friendship and adoration for the big brother, now her brother-in-law, who had taken me under his wing, offered me the opportunity to do the only thing that ever mattered to me – drum. All across the States and Europe.

I loved Lucy like a sister, so it was a safe bet that I should stay away from her actual sister.

After the retreat's party, when I'd spent the evening under the blanket, I thought I'd glimpsed a sense of the woman Elle could have been in my arms.

She needed more, I knew that. She had her mark to make, in a world I had no desire to be part of; the only time I'd ever worn a suit was to Cain and Lucy's wedding, which had been at his parents' guest house in Cornwall, overlooking the Atlantic Ocean, surrounded by love.

It was also the place where I'd last seen Elle, and the scene of so many memories she'd evoked in me, since I'd had to pull her limp body from the ocean, just before she had been about to embark on her US adventures. In the four years she had been in Boston she had worked during the holidays. The only time she'd visited, when Lottie was born, I'd been in San Diego. I associated her wild personality with the wild Atlantic, and that was my fault. She was more of a city dweller than I'd ever be.

So, I'd booked an earlier flight to San Diego to catch up with Uncle Eddie and some friends. A couple of weeks surfing on the West Coast would give me the head space I needed.

I dove into the Pacific Ocean as the sun set.

Elle didn't need me in her life.

A few days battered by the surf ought to convince me of that.

Driving up to Uncle Eddie's house always felt like I was instantly home, no matter how long it had been between visits. Too long, this time. The two-storey house was set a little back from the ocean, offering stunning views and privacy, which was why he and my Aunt Issy had decided to buy the place in the late 90s. Their plans to have a family had never happened in the way they'd expected though – instead of having babies and toddlers to dote on, I turned up as a distraught twelve year old. Only five years later Aunt Issy was gone, too. Eddie had never remarried. The death of his sister and his wife in just a few short years would have closed off a part of my heart, too.

I parked on the drive and headed around to the back, where I knew Eddie would have the grill going. I put the beers in the cooler and hugged the man who embodied music and the ocean.

'Good waves out today?' He asks, turning the fish on the grill. Lime and salt filled the air and it was like I'd never been away, despite it being over a year since my last visit and that was only a quick weekend after an LA show.

'The swell was so good. You should come with me tomorrow.'

'I might do. My project can wait a little longer. It's not every day that my favourite nephew turns up.'

'Blame it on the music, Unc. Lucy and Cain are expecting again, so this is the calm before the storm of finishing up his new album.'

'A family should have lots of children.' He smiled, brushing the fish with a little homemade peppered oil.

I settled our new beers on the table and sank back into one of the chairs. 'What property are you working on now?'

'Oh, a little place up the coast. Couple bedrooms, stunning views. Big rooms for entertaining children. Maybe you need a west coast hangout?'

'Sure, I'm right here.' I raised my beer and patted the back of the chair. We both knew what he meant, and we both avoided the topic of me extending his family.

After dinner, I connected the speakers to my phone and played a new song Cain had sent me, a mid-tempo number with a seventies feel, which sent us reeling back into the musical archives, reminiscing about seeing The Who, Fleetwood Mac, the Eagles, all across California. Everything I learned about music I learned from Uncle Eddie, when he handed me my first guitar for my thirteenth birthday. I lasted six months before I discovered the drums, thanks to my school's music department. Within a weekend I had a drum kit in the guest room, and every meal time was taken up discussing the techniques of The Who's Keith Moon, Queen's Roger Taylor, Led Zep's John Bonham, Cozy Powell, the Eagles' Don Henley and Dave Grohl – who swapped the drums and made a decent guitarist and front man for the Foos, after the death of Kurt Cobain. Each of the drummers offered something to make them all equal in my eyes.

Uncle Eddie had driven us all around California for live music. Aunt Issy stepped in occasionally when we racked up four nights on the run during spring and fall – key school assessment dates - even though she knew I studied in the car; discussing music offered a lot of English and math opportunities, not to mention the geography of roaming around the state, history and musical appreciation.

Then Aunt Issy became sick, and we stayed home, balancing school work on the drive to hospitals. She didn't see me graduate, but she knew I'd do well, and knew I had to be in Austin or Nashville, nowhere near the coast.

And Uncle Eddie had known that I had to get lost in middle-America for a while. He flipped a dime and heads saw me book a flight to Nashville. Didn't matter that country musicians had guitars, my drums would set fire to the bars on Broadway. And they did.

Over the next few blue-sky days we settled into a routine of surfing in the morning and grilling in the afternoon, all to a backdrop of decades of music. Friends from high school came over to catch up, and Eddie's card buddies came over on weekends and we played long into the morning.

One afternoon Eddie asked me how my search for the elusive Mrs Jam was going.

'I can't believe Cain told you that. But there's no one that can handle this drum-playing traveller.' I smiled. 'How about you?'

He smiled broadly. The coyest I'd seen him since he'd worked out with Aunt Issy how to see a gig six nights a week on the approach to my sixteenth birthday.

'Okay, who is she?'

'Well, Melinda has been a friend for a long time.' He began. 'She helps me show properties when they're ready. Her husband passed a few years ago. He was a good man. Carpenter by trade.'

I nodded. Uncle Eddie put faith in people who could work with their hands. He appreciated a deep discussion, too, but taught me there's nothing like working hard to make playing hard a lot more fun.

'Anyway. Melinda has asked if we could all have dinner one night?'

'Sure. I'd like to hear her thoughts on music.'

Eddie visibly lightened,

'I think you'll find that Mel has been to as many shows as we did, back in the day. We were probably at the same ones without realising it.'

The next morning Seb rang me to ask if he and Sarah could visit, more out of politeness than request; Uncle Eddie had always had an open house. They'd driven across from Nashville, seeing the country, and they wanted a few days by the Pacific before they drove through more deserts.

I helped Eddie make up the guest room, so that they could feel solid ground beneath their feet for a few nights. My drum kit was moved across to the rooftop garden and Eddie and I traded licks as the afternoon wore on.

I was in a sixties jazz mind when I saw Old Blue pull up. I increased the bass and kept the rhythm going, and, sure enough, moments later Seb was on the patio, opening his Martin acoustic guitar. Sarah and Eddie turned up with drinks, and we found our way to everyone's favourite musical decade, the seventies. They joined in on harmonies on Take it to the Limit and Tequila Sunrise as the sun faded behind us.

'Beer?' Sarah rhetorically suggested and we stepped down from our impromptu stage, and she passed us cold ones.

A deck of cards turned up, and we played into the early hours of the morning. I was so relaxed I could almost feel myself readying for Nashville again. But there was no way I was climbing into a van with the second most coupled-up couple I knew, who finished each other's thoughts and sentences only marginally slower than Lucy and Cain.

I agreed to take Sarah and Seb on a tour of San Diego's finest beaches, taking in Torrey Pines and Blacks for the stunning views of sky and rock and surf, winding our way south to La Jolla, where we spent the rest of the afternoon. Whilst they don't hit the waves like me or Cain, they appreciate the sun, a cocktail and, in the case of Sarah, a good book.

By mid-September the crowds of tourists had gone, so we had a good spot in our waterfront bar. It would take Sarah and Seb another five days to drive back to Nashville, thereabouts; they were both happy to wander when necessary. Cain wasn't expecting us for another fortnight, until he'd ironed out some lyrics, probably with Lucy's help.

'There's something so peaceful about just staring at an ocean,' Seb said.

'Absolutely. Spent half my life in the water.'

'You off to Thailand again this year?'

I nodded, sipping my Mojito.

'Mid-November. I reckon six weeks locked in a studio with Cain and I'll be ready for tormenting my body with the waves again.'

We all raised our glasses to our work ethics.

Eddie messaged me and asked if it was okay if Mel came for dinner. She had been excited when he'd told her of our impromptu performance, playing her favourite music and was really looking forward to meeting me.

I replied, grinning at his unexpected, but much-needed, goofiness and we finished our drinks. Sarah made us call into a diner for coconut pie and orange cake, and Seb and I called into a convenience store for more beers. Seb spent a little time looking at the wine, finally settling on a couple of reds and whites he wasn't too unhappy with.

Mel is wonderful. She isn't unlike Sarah, in her relaxed attitude to life and love of music and good company. I could tell Eddie had fallen hard for her, but was trying to hold back. They sat together on the sofa and next to each other around the dinner table, but they were both shy about any other physical displays of affection. I was used to seeing Seb and Sarah drape their arms around and across each other, and Lucy and Cain were often foreheads together laughing at some private joke, stealing kisses in and around family life.

Mel had great taste in music, too, and kept requesting some of my favourite tracks for me and Seb to play. She is big on English rock bands, especially British sixties band The Kinks, and we ended up playing Sunny Afternoon more than a few times.

I went down to the kitchen for chips and dips. Eddie followed me in. It was written all over his face that he wanted to know what I thought about Mel.

'Mel is a wonderful woman – warm, great sense of humour, and as for taste in music? It's almost as good as her taste in men.' He smiled and relaxed. 'I'm pleased for both of you.'

We hugged, and he showed me where he hid the good chips.

The next afternoon Seb and Sarah drove off, hoping to catch sunset at the Joshua Tree National Park, channelling their own inner sixties musicians. I took to the waves and then took Eddie out for dinner and a gig. Two bachelors, now one, out enjoying the evening, in a town where music and the waves are loved in equal measures.

3
Elle

September

As soon as my feet reached the ground at Logan airport, I strode easily through the arrivals hall. Happy to be on familiar ground, I dived towards the first cab in the queue, ahead of an exquisitely tailored suit. I reached the handle a fraction of the second before he did, and offered him a stunning smile before I slipped inside the cab, leaving him on the pavement. I snapped out my address as I settled into the back of the warm leather seat, scrolling through my phone as we wound our way through to the city and my awaiting apartment.

I couldn't wait to resume my life.

I lined up a hair appointment and an express mani-pedi for this afternoon, and then scrolled through my contacts for a dinner date. We'd hopefully go to the cute French bistro overlooking the square, and possibly for cocktails afterwards.

We drove through Cambridge, past the gallery where I'd finally start working as a paid member of staff on Monday. Lights shone above the two modern art pieces in the window. This was why they'd hired me. The lurid green may have caught people's attention but they continued walking, instead of entering one of the most serene rooms that I'd ever spent time in. A former printing works, the space was enormous, but your eye was drawn to the printing press in the corner, which became part of the exhibits, if Fion was of the right mood to listen to me. He would be on Monday, and those eyesores in the window would be replaced with pieces reminiscent of Lowry's stick figures. I was in no way home sick for Manchester, but the new artist would thank me when I used my historical knowledge to curate her first exhibition in the middle of October.

The cab pulled up on my street and I handed over the fare, whilst sidestepping out onto the pavement.

The driver positioned my case on the kerb and wished me a good day before driving off.

The smell of coffee from the two local cafes, and the calm of the cosy women's boutiques, where I spent most of my non-working time, brought a huge smile to my face. I was home.

My apartment was on the third floor of a brownstone, just a few minutes from the Business School I had spent almost a fifth of my life in. Zed, my some-time classmate – he turned up to classes when he thought his visa would be revoked – had found the room for me through one of his many friends. The only thing I heard was discount, and I signed as soon as I could after graduation. I had dreaded living too far away from everything, and having to rely on public transport. Boston is the perfect walking city, just like Manchester.

My rooms were small, but thanks to clever storage solutions, and lots of advice from Zed when he came to visit, I was able to accommodate all my clothes and bags and books and gorgeous kitchen crockery and utensils. My bedroom was my favourite room in the apartment, featuring a queen-sized bed in the centre and floor-to-ceiling storage.

Below the window was a huge sycamore tree which I couldn't wait to watch change colours during the seasons.

My bathroom held a decent shower and sink, and all my favourite luxurious lotions and potions. I turned on my Saturday night playlist on my phone and spent the next two hours beautifying my already gorgeous hair, body and face. To finish, I doused myself with my favourite Guerlain scent. I know how to be remembered.

Halfway through dinner, however, I knew meeting Didactic Daniel had been a mistake.

When I was a final year student I'd enjoyed listening to his tales of his financial job, but, maybe because of my newly-graduated status, I could see he was actually very dull. And he quite liked demonstrating how powerful he was in meetings. If anyone interrupted me with hand gestures during a presentation it would be the last time they ever did. He was definitely buying dinner.

I couldn't remember the last time we'd met, but sat across from him now, struggling not to yawn, I knew I wouldn't be ordering dessert. And they baked the most delicious lemon tarts.

'I said, are you finishing that?' Didactic pointed a fork at my plate. He was either after my salad garnish or the half-finished steak.

I was as done as either.

'Do you know what? I think this evening is finished. You're welcome to my steak.'

I knew he hadn't paid attention to anything I'd said all evening; he only looked up, as I stood, retrieving my bag from the hook under the table, the half-hoiked steak suspended between plates.

'Are we going?'

Bless, he was probably a very nice guy. For someone else.

'I am, Daniel. Simply awful headache, you know?' It didn't do to burn bridges. 'Please, stay and enjoy dinner. I'll order a cab.'

He looked so conflicted that I left before he had a chance to become chivalrous and offer to drive me home.

The air was still warm as I walked along the square towards a cab rank. It seemed a shame to call it a night so early. I peeked into a bar to see if anyone I knew was around, but it was mostly loud Freshers, which I didn't need. I took out my phone to see where people had checked in on the socials. I passed a bar I didn't go in very often, the door opened and I caught the notes of an acoustic set. I put my phone in my bag and stepped inside the room. If the last four weeks in Nashville had taught me anything it was to recognise good musicianship.

The guitarist stood on a stage tuning up. Tables at the front were full, but I found a seat near the bar and waited for another song.

'Can I buy you a drink?' I turned to the flannel shirt before me.

'That was fast, even for a country boy.'

I liked his laugh, and his forearms; he was used to the outdoors, not just an Abercrombie fitting room.

'Aaron.' He held out his hand. 'But my friends call me AJ.'

'Aaron, tell me your favourite country song and we'll see if I'm staying for that drink.'

I silently collected my shoes from the bedroom floor and headed for the front door, careful not to disturb AJ as I slide the chain back, sneaking out like I know he'd want me to. He was still rhythmically snoring and I searched through my bag, heaving a quiet sigh when my rose gold Apple glinted up at me. The morning-after retreat is always mortifying if you have to go and collect your misplaced phone.

The sun was just waking up as I stepped into the Uber. If I was lucky I'd catch a few hours sleep before a late brunch with Zed to find out what shenanigans he'd been up to over the summer in Hong Kong. No doubt it would have involved a lot of shopping, for both of us.

And who was I to argue if he wanted to shower me with gifts?

I met Zed in our favourite coffee shop much later that afternoon.

He was seated at a table, staring into the abyss of an empty espresso cup when I arrived. He immediately stood and we air kissed twice, as if in Paris, and the dramatics began.

'What's up, Zed?'

'My stress levels. In-', he checked his Tag Heuer watch, 'sixteen hours, I have to go to work, Ellie-Roar.' He looked so serious but I couldn't help laughing. Plus, his crazy nickname for me, based on both my surname and empowerment always made me smile.

'You're working in the sales office of a stationery company, overlooking the beautiful Charles River. And your cousin is the MD. Chances are strong that you'll be shopping all day while he offers to fetch your coffee. Refill?'

He grinned then, nodding, as I stepped the short distance to the counter. 'And a piece of pie. Extra cream.'

We both knew I was right about his first day.

After ordering I placed his espresso and my caramel latte on the table, and spotted the oversized gift bag.

I looked at him, questioningly. He beamed and nodded, holding the bag out for me.

'Oh, you're an absolute legend, Zed,' I peered inside the paper bag and found a smooth cotton fabric branded bag from my favourite store. Inside the protective bag I gently lifted out a gorgeous, buttery leather DKNY handbag, in the softest pastel pink.

'We have to look fabliss.'

'Always.' I finished our sentence and hugged him.

I couldn't wait to go to work tomorrow.

I just managed to put the bag away when our desserts arrived, and over the next hour he caught me up on his HK summer. I couldn't believe the contrast between his August and my countrified lack-of-adventures season. Oh, it had been so good to see Lucy, and catch up with family. And I was pleased she'd reached out for me to help her promote the retreat, but I had missed out on a lot of coffee and shopping dates. No matter, I'd make it up, now that I was home.

4
Jam

Late September

'Come back to bed, Jam.'

I pulled on my shorts, and turned around to face the woman, who was on the final SoCal leg of her gap year – but dammit I still couldn't remember her name.

'I would love to, but the surf is calling me. Come out with me.'

But I knew she was a non-swimmer. She'd never follow me to the ocean.

I'd spent yesterday afternoon surfing, and when I returned to my spot on the sand, a group from a nearby hostel had set up. I watched as various nationalities and abilities shrieked in and out of the water, while I finished my protein snack and drink. One girl had remained on her towel, propped up on bags, a paperback novel in her hands. She wore a large sunhat and oversized sunglasses. Her cover-up covered up plenty on top, but her desert-dry legs were turning a little pink. She'd been nowhere near the water.

I had scooted over to her, grabbing her SPF. She'd peered down her glasses at me, and enough of a smile formed at her lips for us to end up having a really good evening.

I pulled on my top.

'Aren't you scared of sharks?' the woman shuddered, pulling the covers up over her body. 'I'm not scared of sharks' I grinned, leaning down for a goodbye kiss.

I drove back to Eddie's along the coast, noting the last time I'd see the big blue for a while, as surf crashed against the rocks and gulls soared overhead. The stereo remained unusually quiet as I enjoyed the warmth of the afternoon on my arm and face, a slight breeze through the open window tickling my skin.

Each time I left California I'd felt lighter in my mind, recharged and ready to tour. But this time felt, not quite uneasy, but unsure. I had houses in Nashville and Newquay, but they didn't feel like home. Maybe I did need Eddie to find me something in San Diego?

I wouldn't tell him just yet, though. I had a feeling he'd have me with a Californian zip code all of my own before I had a chance to think things through. I was glad he had Mel in his life now. And I wasn't surprised when I returned to find them both on the balcony, a bottle of wine on the table. Eddie found me a glass and poured me a drink, and decided to order Japanese food.

After a sociable hour I made my excuses to head up to my room to finish packing. Mel wrapped me in her arms, promising me she'd take care of Eddie. I had absolutely no doubts that she would; I had enough experience around besotted couples to know genuine affection between people. Even as a young child I'd seen the connection between my parents. More than loving each other, I saw their daily care and admiration

– Dad making Mum's morning coffee, Mum knowing when Dad needed to laugh. It was this bond I needed, and I knew I wouldn't settle for anything less in the woman I spent the rest of my life with.

The following day I checked in to the airport for my flight back to Nashville. I had a couple of hours before my plane departed, so I made a nearby bar my office for the afternoon, listening to a couple of new songs Cain had sent across.

I kept my eyes on the board for my flight, and ordered a steak dinner, so I wouldn't have to cook when I got back. Though Lucy also kept a similar open house to Uncle Eddie, and I knew I was always welcome to raid their fridge for leftovers.

A flight for Boston was announced and I wondered how Elle was getting on in her new job at the gallery. She was probably at her desk the whole day, dealing with phones and clients, socialising at night to secure deals. I couldn't think of anything worse for a career.

Our worlds were so different.

5

Elle

Early October

I was working fourteen hour days in the gallery and I couldn't be happier.

From the moment I unlocked the doors, just after eight o'clock, with my skinny soya double shot latte, and entered the office space, I was who I was born to be. Organised, ordered and on-it. No task was too complex or simple. I especially loved discussing the artist's inspirations with them, over a cocktail or two. That I was from England, and an enthusiastic student of the Romantic period were my two strongest assets. The days wandering around Manchester's libraries and galleries had paid off, even if I'd never left the UK until I'd flown out to Boston, four years ago.

Fion didn't usually saunter through the door until just before 11, hungover from whichever after-party he'd happened to be at, which meant I had almost three hours in peace to plan the launch of a relative unknown artist in the art world, who was fascinated by Lowry's paintings. Tyler Sunny's industrial east coast American interpretations of the shadowy stick figures and Salford factories back home in England were going to be the next best thing in the art world, and I was helping her work find an audience of millions; on opening night I was going to live stream the exhibition across the world.

Before that could actually happen, in just two weeks, I had lists to cross-reference and telephone calls to make, to ensure everything was accounted for.   But, as Cain reminded me each time I mentioned events, Bob Geldof had organised 1985's Live Aid in the same amount of time. I could curate a few eyes on the next big artist.

When Fion entered the gallery this morning, in a heavy, Tom Ford-scented whirl of tweed and denim, he bore bags with cronuts. And coffee. I looked up from the spreadsheet and realised it was almost lunch time.

'Elle-on-earth, where are we with Sunny's launch?'

I stretched out my arms, arched my back and swivelled around to dive into the latte, ignoring another ridiculous nickname, which he thought a witticism.

'Tickety boo, Fi. Caterers have confirmed the menu, including the incredible patisserie board, for less than the price we wanted. Obviously.' I dipped a cronut into the foamy top of my caramel latte, more in need of the sugar hit than I realised.   'Also, Sunny has finalised her VIP guest list, and this afternoon I'm visiting the tech team to confirm software setup.'

'What would I do without you Elles-Bells?' It was a rhetorical question and we both smiled. The gallery would not have brought in its first million, had it not been for the sales I'd brought in over the last twelve months, as a mostly unpaid intern – I was kept in Martini's and lattes and gorgeous goody bags, mind.

I finished lunch and WhatsApp'd several of my best clients to remind them about the launch date, and whispered up their exclusivity. Good old Harvard alumni and four years of networking.

I wrapped my wool coat around me just before three o'clock, said goodbye to Fion and slid into the awaiting Uber, to head towards MIT for the digital meeting. I ordered dinner to be served to Jake and Tim, who I knew would have forgotten lunch. But their enthusiasm for the software they were developing was contagious. We'd be the first gallery to use the application, and the investor possibilities were incredible.

When I reached the office, however, judging by the crowd gathered, either a commotion or celebration was in place. A quick look at the still faces around me suggested the former.

'Tim?' I asked. He shook, and then hung, his head. I scanned the room, realised there were far too many undergraduates in, not contributing to anything except perhaps claustrophobia and I set to work. Within minutes I'd operated the minimalist coffee machine - once I'd located the on switch - for their favourite Costa Rican roast blend, and accepted the food delivery, plonking the pizza on the conference table that was probably half the size of a suburban dining table.

Tim and Jake migrated towards the food, and through our unique collaborative communication I managed to gather that serious investment had been lost.

Which meant the project couldn't be finished.

Which meant my digital launch wouldn't happen.

Oh yes, it absolutely would.

'Elle, we need to secure a hundred thousand to complete.' Tim was so shocked he couldn't quite lift his pizza slice. Jake had no such qualms, but I knew he ate through nerves.

'Listen, lads.' I brought out my best British accent, somewhere between Kate Winslet and Maxine Peake. 'When have you ever known me to back down from a challenge?'

Tim reached tentatively for a slice. I'd ordered extra pineapple for him.

'Remember all those late nights, working together, so well, to ensure our work was the best? I still do that. You have both always been the beautiful minds behind everything we worked on. I close the deal.'

Jake paused in eating his second slice and smiled, 'And you positively PR'd the hell out of the experience.'

It was good to hear them laugh, albeit briefly. I sipped my lukewarm drink. 'Yes, and I still do that, too. Come on, tell me what you need.' I opened up my iPad to make lists.

I'd worked with Tim and Jake since we'd met on a digital skills course in my second year and their third year. When they heard my accent, they started asking about period dramas, which I watched a lot of thanks to Lucy and A Level English. We found common ground in a BBC adaptation of Pride and Prejudice which we watched in our rooms before every project. Externally, they were pretty awkward socially, but I knew no one could match their software skills, and I only ever want to work with the finest people. I always opted to team with them on group work, for our next two years together, and we gained the highest grades in every project.

They had clearly been a couple, but I hadn't asked and they hadn't confirmed. Until their graduation, when an unannounced visit from Jake's Dad saw him literally hiding in my closet. I will never understand how, in the twenty-first century, parents can still be so dim-witted and vile towards their own child. I soothed Jake, while Tim spoke with Jake's Mum and everyone attended graduation. Jake's parents hurried home as soon as they could.

Earlier this year, Jake and Tim had married, in a private ceremony in Vegas, which Zed and I witnessed, on probably one of the most expensive weekends of my life. We all dressed up for dinner, we lost more than we won, we ate huge breakfasts at lunch time and we shared a helicopter over the Grand Canyon together, one of the most incredible sights I've ever seen. I'll never forget the piercing blue sky reflected in the Colorado River as it carved through the orange and red rock.

Life becomes particularly fraught for Jake and Tim from Halloween, due to the impending family-heavy commitments of Thanksgiving and Christmas. Their parents know they're married, but it's best to limit time with Jake's parents. Tim's family over-compensate, and that's just as unbearable for two of the quietest men I know. I wish we'd had Sunny's launch in the spring.

And Halloween had arrived early this year, it appeared, thanks to their sudden financial loss clashing with their nerves. However, with the list of practical tasks we'd deciphered between us, I was determined to raise the funds in the next few days. For the two men who helped me understand the academic world in a way I perhaps wouldn't have.

It was almost midnight, my voice hoarse from telephoning everyone I knew with money, by the time I sank into bed and my crisp white Egyptian-cotton sheets. Four days left.

6
Jam

Early October

'San Diego was beautiful, man.' I wound up Cain.
'But you're a family man now, no time for the ocean anymore.'

Cain laughed, but we both knew he would be in the waves faster than a Texas two-step if he wanted to be.

Say if Lucy and Lottie were on a beach.

But he was just as at home in the mountains of Tennessee, creating space for musicians and writers, as he was in the surf.

And working on final material for album three, which is what we were attempting to do now.

'Okay, okay, no more beach talk.' He called. 'Now, I've invited a couple of song writers to join us today. They should be here soon. So, show me what you have musically.'

We ran through a couple of songs then Lucy opened the door, followed by two women. The first, a brunette, carried a guitar case over her shoulder and easily shook Cain's hand, then mine, introducing herself as Patty. Behind her followed a taller woman, long, blonde hair resting on the upper pockets of her denim jacket. She carried a keyboard case, and shook our hands equally as easy, stating her name as Bonnie. As the writers set up their equipment, Lucy hovered nervously, her eyes following Patty in the most star-struck way. I'd never seen her like that around Cain, even in their early days.

'Patty, Bonnie. Thank you both so much for coming today.' He held Lucy's hand, their fingers entwining.

'Thank you for inviting us.' Patty smiled, and Bonnie agreed, her smile so natural, so enticing.

'I have to say, Patty, it was my wife, Lucy, who brought your song to my attention, Murdering Carolina.'

Lucy nodded, and I don't think she could have spoken, even if Lottie walked in the room. Cain continued, 'So of course I had to look up my wife's favourite song.'

'Well, thank you, Lucy, I'm glad you liked the song.'

I saw Cain gently release Lucy's hand, nudging her forward. I helped Bonnie set up her keyboard.

'I love the imagery you created, of a murder-with-intent, with just the right amount of words to have the maximum impact.' Lucy gushed. 'I heard it on a UK radio station, but then I never heard it again, and I just kept waiting. Thankfully, the images stayed with me and I looked you up online, and was so impressed with your album. I played it to a few of my students, to demonstrate language techniques.'

'Why, thank you so much, Lucy, I'm so glad I brought the story to life for you so that you could share it.'

'And that is why my wife is the driving force behind Nashville Narrators.' Cain smiled, tuning up his guitar.

'Well, I'll leave you all to your work.' Lucy said, her hand on the door handle.'

'You can stay if you want to, sweetheart?'

'I'd likely monopolise all of your time.' She smiled. 'Besides, Lottie's napping which means I'm lesson planning. I'll stop by later.'

'Okay. Love you.' He smiled at Lucy, tuning his Gibson Hummingbird as she left the room.

Bonnie's back straightened and she stared straight at Cain.

'I am so freakin' glad that Sarah pestered me to stop by. I honestly did not peg you as such a smart man.'

'Smart?' I echoed.

'No sass and all of the class.' She elaborated. 'I respect genuine connections and accreditations.' Bonnie turned to her set up, began playing a song from Cain's first album, Late Night Drinking. Cain and Patty picked up their guitars to join in and I sat behind my kit ready for the beats.

Although they couldn't stay for long, I had a feeling we'd see more of Bonnie and Patty on future albums, their reflective storytelling working harmoniously with the rough stories Cain created. Bonnie's keys enhanced the songs, and both women had wicked humour, trading memories as if they'd worked together all their twenty adult years, instead of just meeting on the journey over here.

After a couple of hours we wound up the session. Lucy had been by on a break from her own writing, silently sitting and watching, enjoying the music-making process, then left as the video monitor indicated Lottie was waking up from her nap.

Cain and I worked on a couple of songs for another hour, and Lucy came by again. She held the coffee pot and beers up to us, with a question in her eyes. We opted for coffee; the beers would wait until these final two tracks were cut for the day.

As she settled the coffee on the table, Cain stood to embrace her, the move instinctive. She nestled into him for a few minutes; their heart beats almost one, after just an afternoon apart, his hand softly smoothing her growing baby bump. I'd never really paid much attention to their movements as a couple, but in this small space, it was all I could see. Their touches mirrored each other; Lucy settled under his arm, her arm around his waist. Their free hands held lightly, as they discussed Lottie, how Lucy was feeling, how the album process was going.

I turned my back to offer privacy on the tender moment, sipping my coffee and intently studying a crack on the wall. After a few minutes I realised Lucy had been speaking to me. I turned back around, smiling, the beating of my own heart settling. I needed just half of what they had, although it would never be possible.

'Hmm?' I smiled.

'Are you staying for dinner, Jam? I've fought with a turkey and seem to have won.'

Did I want to return home to an empty house? Did I want to encroach on their family time? But I knew these guys so well I knew they'd be offended if I didn't help to eat the plentiful dishes I knew Lucy would have cooked.

'That would be amazing, thank you.' I knew Thanksgiving preparations had begun, and how nervous Lucy was at feeding the inevitable throng of people that turned up throughout the day. Most of the time meals were simple affairs, but there were certain meals Lucy rolled up her sleeves for and threw herself into. By her own admission she was not a cook, but when she did create, it was just another example of her contentment and I never left a table disappointed.

Cain and I went back to the album tracks, finishing up just before dinner.

'Wow.'

'I know, right?' I grinned. 'We'd normally only be waking up around now, never mind finishing for the day.'

Cain nodded. 'Do you miss the road?'

'A little. I miss playing every night, but I don't miss the overnight cramped journeys.'

'We'll be back out on the road next year.'

I slapped his back, 'I know that, man. You and Seb are about as likely to give up touring as I am. But, family first. In whichever capacity you go out on the road, we're right here with you, even if that means you only play Nashville shows. Although I'm sure we'll be hitting England as part of this tour?'

'Oh, definitely, man, my parents would disown me if I didn't visit at least once a year. Sarah's finalising the UK bookings for the summer, just after CMA Fest in June.

We packed away and Cain headed up to the main house while I worked out a few kinks on the drums.

I was driving my way through some seventies funk when I caught a woman watching me through the glass. Her face was pale and round, almost like a new moon. Her smooth red hair settled at her neck. I ducked my head down to finish the beat and when I looked up again she'd gone.

I climbed out from behind the kit and went to wash up for dinner.

7
Elle

Mid-October

As calmly, and gently, as I could I replaced the telephone handset, a juxtaposition of professional and giddy emotions fighting for my attention.

I'd secured the last thirty thousand of the funding.

In a twenty minute chat with AJ.

I was so good.

I'd scrolled through all my contacts at least once, and paused on AJ's number. I didn't remember programming it in, but then he was messing around with my phone in the bar that night. He remembered me when I rang, too, and laughed that a fire engine could roar through his bedroom when he's sleeping and he'd never hear it. No hard feelings about my early departure. And, it turns out he's a very successful tech-nerd, a writer and financially proactive. He understood the issues and suggested fair percentages, which I accepted on behalf of Jake and Tim; this software was the key to another of their projects.

AJ and I were also going for dinner tomorrow.

Before I rang Tim and Jake to share the good news, I burrowed into the feelings of warmth and giddiness that rapidly spread through me. In only a week, through many, many calls and meetings, I'd raised a hundred thousand pounds.

I shot out of my seat and danced across the empty office, to where we keep the good liquor, and poured myself a generous measure of Jameson. I raised my glass, breathing in the moment and the memories and the possibilities. The liquid heat sharpened my focus, the taste teasing my tongue, and I returned to my desk.

I picked up the phone again and called MIT. Jake answered and for the next three minutes I was treated to a series of squeals and yelps that I took to be excitement

I locked up the office and walked briskly along the street, towards home, needing to siphon off the excess energy.

The lights of a cocktail bar caught my eye and I nipped inside the crowded room. A band played nineties covers in the corner, teen spirits entertaining themselves. Students, still in corporate attire, filled the floor. They probably earned a hundred thousand in a year. Or before breakfast. They would have this feeling every single day. Of being in control, of belief in yourself. What would I do if I earned this much as my salary? There was no way Fion would even double my income, even when I sold more of Sunny's work at her launch than he would. Would I travel more? Would I buy more? Probably not, as I genuinely loved the creative environment and the marketing role I'd carved for myself. I wouldn't work this hard in any other boardroom, not until I was running my own gallery on the Cape.

A familiar RnB song started playing and I headed towards the cloakroom.

Welcome to moneyed Harvard, I thought, staring at the racks of cashmere wool coats, as I handed my coat to the attendant, pocketing the receipt in my Tommy Jeans. I looked around the bar, recognising former Law and Business graduates, celebrating, networking. Crafty Christian, someone I shared an accounting class with in the second year, spotted me and beckoned me over. He introduced me to his colleagues as the English girl who broke his heart, but we shared a smile; we'd enjoyed a mutually fun night or two, and that was where it ended. The woman he was with now eyed me up and down several times, clearly uncertain if I was still a threat. No, because Christian was a bit too evasive and mysterious for my liking. Cain was my yardstick - I needed certainty and humour and adventure in a life partner.

I paid for a round of drinks, downed my Vodka shots and headed to the dance floor with a couple of the other women.

I woke to brusque daylight and tentatively reached behind me.

Thankfully, I was alone.

I listened out for the sounds of running water just to double-check there was no one in my bathroom, or kitchen, and smiled when my empty apartment remained just that.

Normally, Saturday mornings would find me in the gallery, especially so close to Sunny's launch. But from the drum solo in my head I seem to have celebrated quite hard last night. I could do with a little calm before the storm of the next week, when I'd rarely see any bed, let alone my own.

I snuggled under the duvet, hoping for a little more sleep, but my stomach growled and my head was desperate for painkillers. I fixed my hangover cure of toast and honey, made a large pot of tea and distracted myself with an online show until my headache subsided. Then I began the beautification required before a date.

As agreed, I met AJ – Aaron John Winters, of the old money New York Winters, I had discovered – at the restaurant, just after 7.30. I'd chosen the Asian-fusion place based on my absolute love of their steamed dumplings and Teppanyaki grill.

He wore dark denims and a dark blue checked shirt, and had trimmed his beard. He looked as good as I remembered, although he surprised me with a full-on mouth kiss in greeting.

I recovered, and ordered wine, and we talked about the project whilst the small dishes came our way. He told me about his brother's financial success that had brought him into investing.

By the time the bill came, though, we'd run out of things to say.

'Your place or mine?' He joked, but the humour felt off. We'd had a good evening. But that was it. The transaction that would change the gallery, change the lives of Tim and Jake, shifted the power between us. I'd be sleeping with him for money.

I lay a hand on his, very solid, bicep, inwardly groaning at what I was about to do.

'Aaron. Nothing can happen between us. Let me pay for dinner, I'll claim it back from the gallery.'

He straightened up and I felt the air cool. I moved my hand away quickly.

'No. I'll pay for dinner. I invited you out. I'd hate for you to feel obligated'.

'Aaron.' I waited for him to look at me, which he reluctantly did.

'I never let bone-shaking sex distract me from a project.' I pulled him towards me for a goodbye kiss. 'But the project is done with in just two short weeks.' I felt his smile beneath my lips, only briefly encumbered by the little white lie. My bones hadn't even trembled.

And this was probably the last time I was going to see him.

The following morning, free of both hangover and regrets, I ran a few laps of Boston Common, then headed to my gym and spa to ready myself for the reason I had remained in Boston.

To launch my name as vital to the art industry and to become a partner in Fion's gallery this time next year. The final step before owning my own gallery.

Sunny was just the first artist of many I was bringing on board, and Fion wouldn't want to miss out on the spoils.

I hadn't slept more than four hours in the last several days, on the lead up to this, launch night.

I was stood in my black Louboutin's and red Dior dress, looking more confident than I felt. I was ready, but Tim and Jake had gone into hiding. They had to be here in person for the tech support. I could only do so much.

People started to arrive, and I welcomed them, handing out drinks. I checked in for the millionth time on Sunny and Fion, and continued to delicately pace the room and message Jake. Again. He'd better be dead or in a cab.

Suddenly a message pinged through from Tim.

They weren't coming. They couldn't do crowds.

Were they fucking kidding me? I'd promised them I'd escort them through the room and into a specially prepared booth, complete with every snack they'd ever mentioned, but specified they would need to work the tech in person. We were an hour from streaming around the world.

I stepped into a corner and rang Tim. To his credit he picked up quickly.

'Jake's having a meltdown. I can't leave him.'

I counted to five, ran my tongue over my teeth and whispered soothings. I understood. But I wasn't able to use the software like they could. I needed them. After a gentle five minutes I could sense my tone rising. But there was no one else, and they weren't coming over. They were very sorry.

They were very sorry?

I shook my head and asked them to talk me through instructions, in very basic language, and asked they email a written copy.

'Problem, Elle's-Bells?' I jumped at the proximity of Fion, and gathered my thoughts before spinning an illness yarn, but that everything was under control. I saw Sunny walking towards us, and fixed my smile even wider, waved, and headed in the opposite direction, to the complicated tech that lay before me. Then inspiration hit and I called the one man I really needed right now.

'Yo, Elle.'

'Jam. Any chance you're in Boston?'

His throaty chuckle sounded like a lavender balm over my stress levels right now.

'Long shot.' I said. 'Anyway. Fancy talking me through some extremely complicated tech putting-together.'

'What's up Elle?' His concern threatened to unnerve me and I crashed on.

'Absolutely boring story. For another time. I'm about to send a picture, if you could make sense of it and talk me through set up, I'd be bloody grateful.'

'No need Elle, we're family. Send it through.'

I rang off, sent as many pictures of devices and ports as I could, along with Tim's written instructions, and tried not to look at the clock. Fion returned and I assured him everything was absolutely fine. If he could ensure everyone had their drinks topped up, then that would be wonderful. He looked dubious but disappeared, even though the caterers we used would be making sure of the same task. If they wanted to continue working with us.

A minute later an edited document came and I swear it would make Jam marriage material for someone. He'd colour-coded equipment pieces and numbered the order each wire had to be set up. Fifteen minutes until live.

Ten minutes later Fion returned, just as I plugged in the last wire. I was bloody grateful this dress didn't show sweat marks. I stood up, brushed myself down, and faced a disgruntled tiger.

'What on earth do you think you're fucking doing?' He stuttered. 'Where the hell are your tech team?' I stumbled back against his vitriol, but quickly recovered.

'Everything is working as it should.'

'If you ruin this, if you ruin me!' I'd honestly never seen a temper tantrum like this. He leaned in towards me and his breath was whiskey-soaked.

'Fion. We're going live in three. We need to gather people.'

'This fucking artist is not worth any mistakes from you, but if you ruin tonight, I will ruin you.'

I nodded that I understood and held out my arm for him to lead the way, letting out a slow expulsion of breath as I crossed the room to the waiting hundreds.

Shock in various poses on each of their faces.

I spun my head towards Sunny. Tears on her face. What on earth?

A waiter approached and whispered in my ear, and my own face crumpled moments before my body shook.

Everything Fion had just said had been transmitted to the whole room, and the art world, via the live feed.

A tornado of nausea kicked in and I fled the crowd before the flood of tears bubbled over, grabbing my oversized bag as I charged through the door.

I felt the phone vibrate in my hand as I walked around Boston, unable to think. Unable to do anything except hyperventilate. I was cross with myself for walking out; if I'd had more sleep I would have recovered in the gallery and Fion would have remembered who he was talking to. But when it had mattered I'd bolted. All my hard work thrown away.

The dark gave way to very dark, and as if coming out of an ethereal fog I looked up to see where I was.

I had absolutely no idea.

Huge brownstone apartments surrounded me, but there were no discernible signs or markings indicating where I was. Why did I take a taxi absolutely everywhere? I'd known every nook and cranny of Manchester based on my savings plan of walking between college and work and home.

I sat on a wall and scrolled through my phone's GPS to pinpoint a location and call an Uber. My body shook again, from the cooling air. This dress was nothing but a beacon for bother.

The phone vibrated again, as I was searching, and I hit the green button by mistake.

'Hey Elle, did everything go okay?'

Jam.

Hysteria was on the way, and I forced a smile. Fake it until I make it.

'Your instructions were brilliant, Jam. I completely put all the equipment together as you said.'

'Good, good, glad I could help. So how did the event go?'

I took a deep breath, steadied myself.

'Can't lie – it was a bit of a disaster. Don't laugh, but I somehow managed to hit a live button that I didn't know existed, broadcasting a conversation that nobody wanted to hear.'

'Oh, I'm so sorry, are you okay?'

'That's a bit of an understatement. And I'm British. Please, don't be kind to me now, just banter.'

'Elle, I'm worried, where are you?'

'Oh, definitely not the Bahamas. Or a pub.'

'If you were in the Bahamas I'd race you to the ocean.'

'And I would so win.'

'Only because I'd let you – so I could watch your terrifically long legs stride ahead of me.'

I smiled, and shivered, glad that no one else was around.

'You're going to have to buy me a cocktail next time we meet for that comment.'

'Absolutely worth it. What are you looking at right now?'

'Plenty of houses. They look lovely. The kind that people have dinner parties in.'

'Have you been walking all this time? About an hour?'

'Hmm, about that.' I said, clutching my arms around me.

'Look up at the sky, Elle, what do you see?'

'Umm, it's black?' I offered.

'Yes, but give your eyes a minute to adjust. Where's the North Star? To your left or right?'

A Level sciences came wandering back and I tried to focus.

'I can see lots of stars. Just looking for the brightest now.' I turned around. 'Ah, it's directly in front of me.

'Bet you wish you were on the couch watching stars on TV, right?'

'Absolutely.'

'Got you Elle. There's an Uber heading towards you. ETA 9 minutes. Want to hear what Cain's had me doing recently?'

'The Macarena.'

'Whilst I do rock a Latin groove, and in correct sequence, I'll have you know, no, he's almost finished the third album.'

'Oh, brilliant. How's it going?'

Jam filled me in, keeping me updated with the Uber arrival. When it was a minute away, a car drove past slowly. I was about to peer in when something seemed off. The window rolled down.

'You looking for a ride, honey?'

'Officer, send a cab to the location I just gave you.' I shouted into the phone.

'Elle?'

The car sped off and I sat back on the wall.

'Couple of likely lads thinking my red dress is some sort of distraction or something.'

'I'm staying on the phone with you until you get home.'

'Who's paying for this call?' The prospect of job hunting loomed.

'I rang you, remember.'

'Then natter away, my friend, natter away.'

'Did you know my name isn't Jam?'

'It isn't?'

'No – wanna guess?'

'Cedric?'

I smiled at his warm laugh, despite the night's craziness.

'Rumplestiltskin?'

'It's James. Logan.'

'Well, James – please tell me your middle name is Theodore – Logan, I think my car is here.'

'Good, and no middle name.'

Thankfully the real Uber had turned up and I stepped in to the warmth, Jam still talking away in my ear. Ten minutes later we pulled up outside my apartment block, and I quickly let myself in.

'Jam, it has been wonderful talking with you, but I'm now safely home, and in need of a huge bubble bath.'

'You're just wishing you were in the Caribbean Sea, aren't you?' He laughed.

'Good night, Jam.'

It was only as I sank into the bubbles that I realised I hadn't thanked him for saving my life.

Again.

8

Jam

Halloween

I walked into the living area of Lucy and Cain's home and stopped dead in my tracks. It looked like there'd been an explosion in the middle of the night, turning everything orange, black and white.

'Happy Halloween!' Lucy sang, hysterically off-key, wearing a bat headband and a witch outfit, including orange and black striped tights. A cute mini bat danced beside her in her black velvet onesie.

'Happy Halloween.' I replied. Cain wandered in, made up as Frankenstein with a bolt either side of his neck. 'I'm starting to feel woefully underdressed.' I declared, laughing. 'Excellent work on the decorations, though, the party doesn't start until later this afternoon, does it?'

'Yep, we're starting officially about three, just wanted to get the most out of the day.' Lucy placed some more ceramic ornaments and hurricane lights around the fireplace, and Lottie thrust her bucket at me.

'Trick or Treat.' She demanded.

'Lottie.' Cain warned, and she smiled sheepishly.

I rummaged around behind me and Cain slipped a candy bar in my hand, which I popped into the orange pumpkin bucket.

'We're working on the album with you dressed like that, are we?' I asked.

'Don't worry, we have a wizard outfit for you. Just in case you hadn't remembered, Lucy loves Halloween, for the gothic romance connections.'

'I heard that. Might not be any treats left for you tonight.' She sassed, walking back into the kitchen with mini bat.

'I love that woman.' Cain declared, as we walked through to the studio.

'No decorations in here?' I asked, knowing full well there wouldn't be.

'No way. Now, where were we up to?'

Just before three we left the studio to get ready for the party, and we could hear the noise as we walked down the corridor.

The house was full of mini Halloweeners and their grown-ups; the first wave of the party had begun. Cain dived on in chatting to people and swapping trays of food with Lucy and I went upstairs to change. Lucy may prefer the traditional frightful costumes, but this was a moment for style. I changed into a dinner suit, left a bow-tie undone around my collar and tied back my hair into a low bun; instant hipster crooner. A look I could dig. I just needed to swap my usual beer for a whiskey glass and carry it around with me all night, trying out my cheesiest chat up lines.

As the sun faded the minis and their grown-ups headed out for trick or treating, and I helped Cain with drinks for the second wave of guests.

Seb and Sarah came dressed as Shaggy and Daphne from Scooby Doo, even decorating their van I noticed, dressing it as the blue Mystery Machine for one night only.

'Love the dedication, man.' I high fived Seb and hugged Sarah, then offered them the green punch Cain had prepared, with who knows what. The man had spent so many nights in bars he could have been a mixologist.

'Cheers.' Sarah took the first sip, nodding in muted approval. Seb went next and needed a whack on the back from Sarah. I sipped and figured there was some kind of food colouring, lime and rum, knowing Cain's penchant for beach cocktails. My eyes stung, but it wasn't too bad.

Bonnie and Patty showed up together, dressed as Kenny and Dolly. As we were chatting about their Nashville histories, Lucy came into my eye line. I waved her over and brought her into the conversation and we were soon joined by Seb and Sarah. A few others stood at the edge, keenly listening to some legendary music moments.

'I knew it was tough being a woman in music, but honestly, we're extending studio space up here.' Lucy declared. 'I have no idea how, but we'll make it work. I can't believe it's still so hard to be a woman in the music industry. You'll always be welcome to write here. Undisturbed; I've done my fan-girling.'

Patty – Dolly – laughed and wrapped her arms around Lucy.

Everyone was chatting naturally, and I moved around the room, catching up with people I hadn't seen since the summer. A woman with white hair, possibly dressed like a character from a Peter Jackson film, took my seat next to Lucy. She wore the same star struck expression that Lucy had worn on meeting Patty for the first time.

As customary, I took to the drums later on, carrying on the crooner guise with some rat pack numbers. I looked how I'd imagined Deano would look if he'd played the drums. Seb joined me on stage, fooling around and falling about like Martin's sidekick Jerry Lewis. Before he silenced the room with a Gibson guitar, like only he knows how. He's the Seb-inator on strings. After our skit, I went into the garden heading for the buffet table under the gazebo, also fully decorated, of course.

'Hey, Dean.' I turn to the voice and I'm greeted with a flapper from the 1920s, in a black, fringed, sleeveless dress, black vamp make-up, with purple lips and hundreds of pearls caressing her throat and dipping down her dress in a dizzying array.

'Well, hello, Roxy.' I provide, lifting a gloved hand to kiss her fingers. Our eyes didn't once break contact.

'I just love that Italian song.'

'That's Amore.'

'The one about the pizza.'

'Even if the US showed more gratitude to the pan dish originally.'

'What?' Roxy leans in closer, her heavily made up eyes clearly not in the mood for nutritional information.

'Want another drink?' I offer.

'I have a bottle of Tequila at my place.'

'Which is.....?'

'A five-minute drive away. If you can drive.'

I nod, placing my half-full glass on a tray and follow her out of the door.

'Not quite the limo of the crooner, eh?' I said, opening the passenger door of my truck for her.

'What?'

What was I getting into? Ah, who needed conversation all the time, anyway?

'Okay, where to?' She gave clear directions, which told me she wasn't too drunk for a hook up. And at least I could leave whenever I wanted.

I left Roxy crashed out under her duvet, a satisfied grin on her lips and quietly left her apartment.

But I wasn't ready to go back to the party just yet, which would still be underway even though it was coming up midnight. Lucy and Cain didn't often throw parties, but they were all-nighters. The last one had been at the end of summer, just before Elle left for Boston.

I hadn't spoken to Elle since she'd had that trouble at the gallery, but she'd have talked her way back into her job. I bet she was at a party in Salem. She didn't just stick to traditional themes for dressing up, either. She'd wear whatever she looked good in. Which could be anything; she only needed to look at you and you were drawn to her.

I'd almost followed her lead last time we'd met, and it would have been so easy, and definitely fun. But then what? I didn't mind if I never saw Roxy again, but Elle was almost family, and there were boundaries.

I pulled up in the parking lot of a Denny's, grateful I wasn't dressed like I was hosting a party for one – I could have just come from a stage.

I ordered pancakes and bacon with my coffee and savoured the quietness of the evening. Though decorated, the room was deserted, except for solo diners like me.

'Miss, do you have a pen I could borrow?' I asked the waitress when she refilled my coffee. She smiled and handed me one from her apron and wandered off to refill other mugs.

I started doodling on a napkin, a beat roaming around in my head, something Cain had said this afternoon about commitment and fun being achievable with the right person. I jotted down a few ideas we could work on next week and continued to look out of the window. The dessert counter caught my eye and I ordered a piece of Boston Cream pie with my next coffee refill. The custard and cake and chocolate weren't the kind of comfort I needed right now, but they helped.

Feeling suddenly worn out, I paid and tipped, then set off for Lucy and Cain's guest room, where I was staying indefinitely while we finished the album.

I woke early enough for a run and managed five miles before my stomach growled. There was only one thing better than a Lucy and Cain all-nighter – the morning after breakfast buffet. I just had time for a quick shower before I missed too much.

When I entered their kitchen-diner the party carnage had long gone, but brunch hadn't.

'Morning, Jam, there's plenty of food, you know the rules.'

'Don't leave anything. Consider it my duty.' I grinned, hugging Lucy and high fiving Cain. Lottie was sat up at the table in her booster chair, wolfing down pancakes. She still wore her bat outfit from yesterday, though I suspect she'd slept in between.

'Have fun last night?' Cain asked.

'I did indeed.'

'We saw you go.' Cain laughed, 'but must have missed your return.'

'Cain, leave Jam alone!' Lucy playfully whacked his arm with the back of her wooden spoon and he caught her in a gentle kiss.

'Yuk, Mummy.' Lottie declared. 'I'm going to marry a girl - they're not as stinky as boys.'

'Non-taken, Lotts.' Cain smiled and I jabbed some blueberries, swiped them through syrup and felt the sweetness exploding in my mouth.

I played tea parties with Lottie while Lucy and Cain caught up on a nap. Apparently I wasn't too stinky to play with, I told her.

'You're my friend, Jam, and you play games with me. So you're not stinky.'

Couldn't fault her logic.

When a refreshed Lucy came downstairs later, I was sprawled out on the sofa, a quiet Disney film on, as Lottie slept on my lap.

'Oh, she's so adorable.' Lucy gushed. 'Thanks for keeping her busy.'

'No worries. She has about as much energy as I do, though, I'll have to channel that into drumming.'

'Only if the drum kit has an off button.'

'Fair enough. Cain still sleeping?'

'Yeah, he's out. I caved and went to bed just after midnight. This little baby is not as much of a party animal as Dad.' Lucy placed coffee down on the small table in front of the couch, before sitting next to me.

'So, how was your night last night?' she tried to ask casually.

I smiled. 'Yeah, I had fun.'

'But?'

'I had fun last night.' I said. I knew she was desperate to see me paired off.

'Well, it is what it is. And you can stay here as long as you want to, you know that, even after you return from Thailand.'

'Yeah, thanks. I mean, my apartment is good, but I don't have twenty-four hour access to Disney films.'

We finished our coffee and watched the rest of The Lion King. Cain joined us just before the end, as Lottie stirred awake.

'I'm hungry.' She declared, and we all heartily agreed.

After dinner, and after Lottie had gone to bed, I sat around the dining table with Lucy and Cain, a half-hearted game of Monopoly in front of us, a fire warming the room.

A message beeped through on Lucy's phone and she pulled her glasses down from her hair.

'What?' She quietly exclaimed.

'Everything okay?' Cain asked.

'Yeah, my Sis thinks she could be on her way to work in Hong Kong.'

'What, Hong Kong, Hong Kong?' I asked.

She nodded. 'I don't think there is another one.'

'Wow, she must really be doing well.' I knew she'd talk herself back into her job – and now she's clearly been promoted.

'I know. I'm so proud of her. When are you going to Thailand? Maybe you could look her up?'

'Hmmm.' I nodded. 'I'm going out in the middle of November, but I can fly through HK. Anything for family.'

'Thank you, Jam.'

9

Elle

Halloween

This was the first Halloween since I'd lived in the States that I hadn't gone to a party.

Fion, as he threatened, fired me, and never mind the missed parties and missed bill payments, I had immigration issues on the horizon. And I didn't fancy a quick marriage to ease that problem.

I'd been to every gallery in Boston, and Fion had blacklisted me. It didn't matter all the hours I'd volunteered and interned, and the success of Sunny's work – despite, or maybe because of the disaster, her sales had rocketed that night. From a PR point of view, her story of supposed humiliation had gone in her favour; she had reached out to me on social media to thank me for my work, which I thought was kind of her, if not financially rewarding.

It was a shame no one wanted to hire the person responsible for the event.

I tried to reach out to contacts, but there was nothing available.

I'd sold some handbags and clothes online, receiving just a fraction of their cost, but I'd at least been able to pay this month's rent. I had no idea yet where I was finding the several hundred dollars I'd need for

December's rent. And I couldn't even find a deposit to move to a cheaper property.

Meals were my biggest problem.

I'd always eaten in either school or work, right back to when I studied in Manchester. I just never learned how to cook and ready meals were ridiculously expensive.

For the last few weeks I'd manage to eat for free by walking around Harvard; at some point on campus there was a conference or an event, with plenty of free food.

But woman was not meant to survive on canapés alone. It was a great opportunity to network, but invariably it was the science faculty or engineering faculty that held these events, and conversations were brief.

I'd sold off everything I'd spent a fortune on over the last four years, at heavily discounted prices. I had the clothes I wore so I wouldn't be indecent outside, or cold, and four years of photographs that thankfully I couldn't sell.

I needed something to remember my youth by. Why hadn't I saved anything since starting work? Why was every penny I'd earned seemingly stored on my bathroom shelf? For a nanosecond I considered scrolling through my phone for a date, just so I could eat a normal meal. But that all felt a bit too Holly Golightly, and we were no longer in the sixties.

I went to bed hungry, again, intent on saving money for rent and woke up late the next morning.

How could it all have gone so wrong so quickly? One minute I'm walking high in heels, the next minute I'm auctioning off genuine Louboutins at fake prices.

I didn't realise how cold the weather was, now that November was here, without the twinkly lights of streets and restaurants to warm me up. From my bed – the warmest place in this apartment – the trees are lit up, taunting me, reminding me that I have nothing. Their prettiness hurts, like raw diamonds cutting against the night sky.

My stomach lurches again. I can't face another noodle dish . What would I do for a Lobster dinner, served overlooking the pretty white lighthouse of the Cape? I'd gone on a visit there with some classmates in our third year and had fallen in love with the seaside village feel. I'd only needed one weekend to make up my mind that this is where I was living one day.

I turn over on the bed, curling up into the foetal position and bury my face in the pillow, wrestling with hunger pangs.

I could see if anyone's around for dinner, hope they'd pay the bill if I paid next time – in about a gazillion years - but how much effort is required? My roots haven't been done since September, when I had been celebrating my new career, and before the tech disaster struck.

Before I lost everything.

I slid off the bed, in search of...something. I'm down, but I'm not out. Or some other such sports metaphor. I could ring Lucy and ask if she'd send me money. But that would mean telling her I failed, and I'm not doing that. I have a bloody Harvard degree. I could, but I choose not to. I choose different.

So what the hell do I choose?

Not noodles for dinner.

I open up cupboards, poke around for anything vaguely different.

Crackers? I bite into the three left in the packet and grimace at the stale taste.

Think of the weight loss, Rawcliffe. Think of....think of...there has to be something out there for me. I'm a graduate, with experience. Doesn't matter if the experience ended badly, it must be a good story for someone.

Maybe I'm just looking at this all wrong.

Sure, I have no money for rent next month, but we're seventeen whole days from the due date. A day can make a difference, right?

I spot half a bar of Hershey's that I'd clearly forgotten about; jackpot! The foil comes away easily, and the bitterness rather sums up how I feel about how I feel. But, y'know, hikers eat this stuff for energy.

I pick up my phone and scroll through the apps. There has to be a way of making money on here. Take care of the cents and the dollars will roll in, right?

For the next hour I'm lost on the internet, applying for any kind of marketing position within walking distance, so that I don't have to worry about subway fares. I complete thirty online surveys and earn myself the credit of a free fast food burger meal, which isn't ideal, but isn't noodles, either.

I stretch out my arms, turning to my window on the world. Sunday night. I could risk going out; no one I know would be out at eight – they'd be at parties or in their expensive restaurant by now.

I pull on my boots, ankle-length wool coat and a woollen hat, so I don't have to style my hair, and add a gloss to my lips. Then I step outside for the first time in four days.

The cold is harsher than I expected, even for November, and I hurry along to the dinner-bearing chain.

'Elle!'

I keep walking, pretend I can't hear my name.

'ELLE!' I can hear Zed shuffling behind me, not-quite-running, but he definitely wants to talk to me.

I turn around, because there's nothing else I can do, all thoughts of dinner on hold.

'Elle, honey, how are you?' We hug and air kiss and I smile.

'I'm good, what's new with you, Pussycat?'

'Oh, what a week. Are you heading to dinner?'

'I was just out for a stroll.'

'In three degrees?'

'Never mind me, what are you doing?'

'Oh, it's too cold here, let's do cocktails and shrimp and you can hear me moan, moan, moan.'

I've always been so comfortable around Zed, but I can't let him know how I've failed. I can't let him see. And I can't pay for anything.

Suddenly he pushes me back, lifts my chin.

'You're thin.' He lifts my hat, studies my hair and nods. 'I'm buying dinner, Elle.' He links his arm through mine, no further questions asked from either of us, as he glides us in to a nearby bar.

The atmosphere is at once noisy and warm and neon. How long has it been since I was in a place that was once so familiar? What a difference a fortnight makes.

The host takes our coats and seats us, handing over menus and noting down Zed's cocktail choice.

'I'll just have water, thanks.'

'She'll have a Hurricane along with that water.' Zed orders. He turns to me and unstructs, 'Talk to me, Elle.'

I can't lie to my oldest friend in the States. Before our cocktails have arrived he's got the full story, of how I failed, at work, at life.

'Honey, you haven't failed. You're still fabliss and still upright.'

I blink back something close to tears, grateful for the glass suddenly placed in front of me, and we clink. An understanding. My stomach loops as I read the menu, the prospect of actual food so close.

Zed chatters on about his week, in the world of procurement – a fancy term for buying, he excitedly tells me - and a waiter takes our order.

'Ever thought about teaching overseas?'

'Lucy is the teacher in the family.'

'All Asians want their kids to learn English – the language of commerce. I mean teaching English as a Foreign Language.'

I can't afford rent, never mind a flight. I make murmurings, as if I'm considering the possibility that I can suddenly relocate.

'I know some companies who'd kill for your persuasive skills.'

'Zed, you do a girl so good, listening to her woes, feeding her, getting her tipsy.'

'And they pay airfare.'

Suddenly I'm interested.

'The shopping in Hong Kong is incredible.'

Thanks to the time zones and the work ethic of Hong Kong, by the time we've finished dessert – the most delicious crème brulee - we've emailed the director of the company Zed knows, and I have a Skype interview scheduled in a few hours. After dinner Zed surprises me with the most genuine hug I've ever known him demonstrate.

'Never be afraid to ask me for help, ever, Ellie-Roar', he smoothes my hair, and I cling on to him for a long time.

'Promise.' I whisper.

He walks me to my apartment, and then calls for an Uber to his family home in Back Bay.

The Skype interview went surprisingly well, despite the daft hour.

I had to pretend to teach the director of the organisation the names of animals – including animal sounds – in a singsong Children's TV presenter voice, but my humiliation only lasted twenty minutes.

I've certainly dealt with longer presentations at the gallery.

However, they apparently liked what they saw, as they've just emailed me a one-way flight ticket to HK, departing in two days.

I have forty-eight hours to pack up the last four years of my life.

Thankfully, Zed agreed to store some things, and one of his colleagues will move in to my apartment.

The job in Hong Kong also comes with accommodation, and a basic salary of a few hundred dollars a month; Zed assures me the shopping prices are negotiable, and he'll message me with the right places to shop.

Shopping has never been further from my mind.

10

Jam

The bus charged across to Kowloon, along the criss-cross of concrete that stretches over the water. Fog has settled in, the hills an emerald green silhouette in the distance. I check my phone for details of Cassie's hotel, and message Cain, to let him know I'm catching up with his sister. Then I message Elle again, letting her know I've just arrived, if she wants to meet up.

It hadn't been too much of a problem to reschedule my flight to Bangkok, so that I stopped over in Hong Kong for a weekend. Cassie was also stopping by, on her way to Shanghai to teach, and we'd arranged dinner tonight in her hotel, not far from the bar district.

I check my phone for replies to my messages, but neither had replied, so I continue to stare out of the window. The South China Sea sits on my left and the mountains of Lantau South Country Park on my right; the bus sweeps us along the concrete artery, to where the cultures of east and west merge.

A message pings through on my phone and I swipe the screen. Cain telling me to hug Cassie, which would be no problem, as I really enjoyed hanging out with her whenever I could. Smart, funny and engaging, she made me laugh with her tales of adventures teaching around the world. Recently, she'd spent time teaching little children in Central America, and now she was on her way to east China to teach Business English to corporations – and then heading back to Central America as soon as she could, to redistribute her wealth. Like her brother, Cassie marched only to the beat of her own drum. But then, so did Nancy and Joe, with their guest house, The Lizard, that they liked to keep mostly free of guests in the summer, so that family always had a place to stay. And their eldest son, Jason, had a similar my-way-or-no-way work ethic, as a home-working, self-employed IT consultant living in an exclusive Cheshire address, so he could spend more time with his family.

My phone vibrates again and I open a photo message from Cassie holding a beer. Looks like she'd already started her evening, at four in the afternoon.

Suddenly, the city of skyscrapers loomed. I could almost feel the energy reach out to me, as we wound our way into a built up Tsim Sha Tsui, where traffic seemingly had a will of its own. From there I'd catch the ferry to Hong Kong Island, and the central district's bars, for my hotel and my evening. I could just about cope with twelve hours in this metropolis and then I was on my way to Thailand and her southern islands tomorrow morning.

Just over an hour later I was checked into my hotel and on my way to meet Cassie for dinner. I'd messaged Elle once more to let her know where we were eating, and locked the door, descending the six flights of stairs two at a time.

The air was warm and Christmas decorations competed with neon on my short walk to the restaurant Cassie had chosen. My hunger dialled up to famished when I walked through the doors to be engulfed by tempting flavours.

A host showed me through the large crowded restaurant to the back, where Cassie sat reading a worn paperback.

'Jam!' She exclaims, standing up to grab me in a hug. I love this woman.

'Cass-Cass, you are looking well. I love your new blonde hair.'

'Thank you, I fancied a little change.' She tousled her new style and sat down, putting her book away.

Tea arrived in a pot for me and a glass was upended for the hot liquid to be poured in. I raise my glass to Cassie's and sip the green tea.

'So, not a place I thought I'd see you in, Jammy.'

I nodded, 'A few people I know are in town and I thought it'd be rude not to stop and say hello, when our paths are so close. When are you off to Shanghai?'

'I'm on the late train tonight, and I'm being picked up in the morning by a director of the company I'm working for.'

'Fancy.'

'Essential.' She acknowledged, then, with a wink, 'I'm worth it.'

She orders a range of dishes for us in the local dialect and I asked her for a few of my favourite foods – a steamed tofu and chilli dish I'd remembered, from a great place in San Diego I used to visit, and roast pork.

There was nothing pretentious about Cassie at all. Confident, skilled in several languages and with the biggest heart to share her love with. But I'd never seen her with anyone close in her life, come to think of it.

'How's life for you, Cass?'

'I'm ready for a few months of hard work, and possible investment.'

'What about personally?'

The dishes began to arrive, and we thanked the server, who poured more tea for us.

'I won't be heading back to Cornwall this Christmas. Mum and Dad are sort of used to me being everywhere else, though. And know why I'm doing what I do.'

'Yeah, but won't you be on your own?'

'In China? Are you kidding me?'

'You know that's not what I mean.' I smiled.

We concentrate on the flavours of our food for a few minutes.

'I keep myself entertained, Jam, no need to worry about me. I haven't yet met the person to clip my wings for.'

I finish my mouthful of rice.

'Maybe the right person won't want to clip your wings?'

'So true.' She laughs, and for the rest of the meal we discuss everything else that had been going on in our lives.

'You have a great nose for finding amazing places to eat in.' I sigh, sitting back, thoroughly sated.

'You can't go wrong with a crowded restaurant at meal times. Time for a beer before my train?'

'Absolutely.'

We enjoy a few beers before she heads back to her room for her luggage. I wait in the lobby, watching fish swim in a pond. No new messages on my phone. But I don't feel like I want to go to bed. The beer has given me a buzz for adventure.

I walk Cassie to the station and hug her goodbye, promising to try to catch up more often. Then I thread my way through the amplified streets, waiting for a bar to catch my eye.

One that would be amenable to a friendly drummer, maybe.

11
Elle

Early November

Just over a week ago I had packed a backpack and my biggest suitcase, containing the only essentials I had left, and I flew to Hong Kong.

Just over 48 hours after completing surveys so that I could afford dinner.

The world keeps turning, I guess.

I'd emailed Lucy to let her know I was on my way to Hong Kong, and she thinks this is part of a promotion. How could I tell her otherwise? And I don't really know what 'this' is. This could be a month away to recharge my batteries, until I earn enough for a return flight. Maybe there'll soon be an email from Fion, finally apologising for being an arse and begging me to return.

Perhaps he'd have an ego transplant first.

So, until either of those moments happened, I was in one of the biggest cities in the world and I had never felt more disoriented.

I hadn't quite believed Zed when he'd told me about the shopping in Hong Kong, but it is almost possible to shop for twenty-four hours.

Except, I was working twelve of those each day; I guess that's why the shops have to stay open until after six pm – the usual closing hours back in the UK - and why they held night markets, which remain open long after I've wandered off in search of sleep.

My assistant, Bamboo - a high school student, from the school I'm working at - is leading me along stall after stall of lurid plastic and shiny and cotton and fragranced goods, pushing people aside so I can see a myriad of colours. I have no money and no space to store things. The quality looks dubious, too. Absolutely accurate in visual presentation, but I didn't wander the US malls for four years without spotting a cheap imitation a mile off.

I ask her about food and I'm shoved along to a row of noisy food places. I don't recognise anything, so I just ask for something sweet and full of carbs ... which takes a little help from Google to translate.

In front of me sits a bowl of three small, white buns, lightly steamed, with a little dish of something resembling thick milk on the side. I watch Bamboo collect a bun deftly with chopsticks, swipe through the sauce and pop the bun into her mouth. She's about to ask for a fork for me, when I pick up my chopsticks, my Manchester heritage surging awake. All those late nights in Chinatown with friends were good for something.

I ask if we can leave shortly after dinner, and I return, alone, to my one bedroom high rise apartment. My view is of other high rise apartments, so I spend a lot of time with the curtains drawn, their orange glow giving off an eerie vibe. Everything about the city is fast and frenetic, and I expect my mind will catch up at some point.

Unable to sleep I sit up and drag my trusty laptop over to the bed. I update my status to In Hong Kong and AJ sends me a thumbs-up. The man I managed to secure thousands in investment from. There's no way I'm telling him I've ended up teaching young children.

How can life change so suddenly in a few weeks?

I scroll through my phone and upload images of the food and the night markets I took earlier. Nosing around on his profile I see he's a prolific writer. His high-brow articles are insightful and funny, but I'm not interested in the world of business at the moment. I'm still sore from my sudden disconnection from the elite world I'd spent so much time cultivating.

I spend the rest of the weekend trying to settle to a task, any task, but I can't.

I download an ebook I've wanted to read for a while – escapist romance – but my mind doesn't take to it. There's nothing at all wrong with the writing, more that my concentration levels are fractured.

I wash my hair twice, for something to do, and flick through the television regularly, in the hopes for a show I recognise, but there isn't anything apart from a slapstick comedy about Chinese football players who are good at martial arts. I step outside to go for a walk, but there are too many people, so I retreat back inside.

I'm almost grateful when Monday rolls around again, and I have a purpose.

Except, I haven't worked this hard since being in the gallery as an unpaid intern.

I've never been around so many little kids, and they all keep gazing up at me and giggling. Parents hover at the back of the classroom, watching my every uncomfortable move, and there are at least three teachers at any one time trying to teach...something.

Then every time there's a meal break, there's a meeting. And a post-work meeting.

This job is really not for me.

I thought I'd worked hard at the gallery, but here they're after blood.

Surely it will get better?

I can't moan to Zed anymore, he's been such a rock.

By Friday, my first pay day, I'm feeling really homesick. I message Lucy to update her on Hong Kong. I'm in my bland apartment, exhausted and I just don't want to be near anyone. But I miss being with familiar people. Instantly her face appears on my phone and I click the green icon

'Hi Sis.'

'I can't quite believe you left Boston!'

'Calculated spontaneity.' I reassure her.

'Yeah, but are you happy?'

Yeah, I'm not replying to that. I stretch out on the bed in the day-glow orange room.

'I'm just jet-lagged, Sis. Life in HK is so frantic I don't think I ever had time to recover from the flight. The food is amazing. I don't always know what I'm eating, but it tastes great. How are you doing? How's pregnancy?'

'Oh, better. Back pain is back, but Cain's so sweet rubbing my back every time he sees me looking uncomfortable.'

I sit up straight at the tone in her voice.

'Lucy?'

'Oh, hormones are horrible at the best of times.'

'But?' I wait until my sister talks through what's on her mind.

'I'm just being silly.'

'In what way?'

'Oh, I love having a full house. But lately I'm not sure I know everyone. And it's probably just my imagination but there seems to be more women around, too. And they're so skinny, and, and awake; I nap almost every afternoon.'

'Well of course, you're growing a tiny human.' I smile, lying back down. 'Do you need me to remind Cain how much he loves you?' I can almost see her shake her head, instead I hear the lightness in her voice, which is the next best thing.

'Oh, hang on, there's someone at the door.' I calculate the time difference...it must be just after seven in the morning there.

'Anyway, enough about me.' Lucy sounds too bright when she returns. 'Have you heard from Jam?'

'I think I had a couple of missed calls from him. Everything okay?'

'Yeah, he's in HK, now. Thought you could meet up.'

'I meant with you, Sis. Who was at the door?'

'Oh. Someone with a gift. For Cain. It's nothing, it's nothing.'

'Lucy.' I warn.

'It's just a book for him. About an obscure country artist.'

'Bit early for a delivery.'

'Celene dropped it off.'

'And she is....?'

'Truthfully, I'm not sure. She just sort of appeared.'

I bolt up. 'Lucy.'

'She's harmless. Has helped out with a few errands, I think. Only looks about sixteen. And so pale. I'm always palming healthy bakes off on her.'

'Just be careful, Lucy.'

'You need to stop watching crime films. So, are you going to meet Jam?'

'Might be good to catch up with someone I know'. I can fake success for a couple of hours.

We chat a little while longer, and I ring off, immediately trying to call Jam, but there's no answer. I message him, so he knows that I know he's in HK. Unable to stay inside any longer, though, I send out a message to a couple of the other expat teachers, who have been here a year, and they're up for a night out. Apparently we're heading to the Lan Kwai Fong area, which is where all the bars and restaurants are. I text Jam to let him know where we're going, but there's still no answer.

It feels like a lifetime since I've been in a bar.

Gina and Lily, both from Newcastle, have convinced me I need to karaoke, at the best bar ever, and I've had just enough beer to not argue.

This neon-crazed room is nothing like I imagined it would be. There are several rooms with private karaoke parties, and I've left Gina and Lily and their new friends in one, so that I can have a change of scene.

Suddenly, live jazz music bursts out into the main room. From the bar mirror I can see the lower part of a stage with a drum kit. I order a Hurricane and the beat catches my attention.

Is that?

I spin around in search of the stage. In search of the music. In search of the musician.

Of all the bars, in all the world.

What on earth is Jam doing here?

12
Jam

Mid-November

There's nothing like playing percussion jazz from the fifties and sixties to realign my mind.

I could play for hours, as long as the bar stays open. Great rhythms, played my way.

But I do need a break.

I finish off Brubeck's *Take Five* and announce I'll be back in ten.

As I reach for my beer, a pair of denim-clad legs approaches.

Legs that could only belong to one person.

I look up and Elle is staring back at me, her hands on the waistband of her blue jeans.

'Of all the bars, in all the world, eh, Jam?'

'Indeed. Can I buy you a drink?'

'Absolutely. Grasshopper.'

I follow Elle to the bar. Suddenly, I might not be drumming all night.

'I can't believe you're here! I was texting you all night.' Elle shouts over the dance music now playing. I lean in closer to hear her properly, and wonder if that was wise.

'I'm on my way to Thailand. To teach. You just missed Cassie.'

'Cassie's here as well?' Elle's face is so close to mine. Someone bumps me and I put my hand out on the bar to steady myself so I don't crash into Elle.

'She was. We had dinner, and she's off to Shanghai tonight.'

'Wow. It's a totally different world out here, isn't it?' I nod, sip more of my beer.

'What are you doing here anyway, and not in Boston?'

'I fancied seeing what all this travelling is about.' She smiles, but her eyes look miles away.

'How are you finding HK?'

She pauses, considering her answer.

'It's so very different. Bigger and noisier and brighter.'

'There are pockets of quiet everywhere, Elle, you just have to look.'

'Thanks, Jam.' Her smile is small, but genuine.

'Can I play you a song?' I find myself asking.

'Oh, umm, I'm not sure.'

'Something from England?'

'Yeah, that would be good.' She presses her hand over her heart. 'Thank you.'

I nod, already thinking of the upbeat music I can have her dancing to, and I down the rest of my beer. I wander through the crowd and make my way back to the kit, torn between wanting to play, and knowing that Elle's in the room.

I wonder if her eyes her on me?

I start with Led Zeppelin's *Whole Lotta Love*, replicating the distinctive bass sound from the

seventies rock legends. More people move to the
floor.

Keeping the groove going I dive straight into ACDC's
Shook Me All Night Long and a crowd at the front start
singing the chorus, turning to face the full bar. I spot
Elle definitely having a good time, dancing along to the
beats, in her own world. Then I ramp things up with
The Who's *Baba O'Riley*. My breathing heavy, my arms
numb, I feel a slight sonar shift within me. Then
someone passes me a beer and I down it, grateful for
the quench, and while the crowd recovers I play the
sixties classic *Wipe Out* to cool down.

As the last beat plays I thrust my drumsticks in the air
in a 'that's all folks' movement and climb off stage to
applause, moving through the crowd to find Elle. She's
stood at the bar with a couple of fruity looking drinks,
her eyes never leaving mine.

We clink glasses and I drink half. Pineapple, coconut
and rum.

'You're incredible.' She enthuses.

'Nah, incredible is Thailand, Elle. Crystal clear waters.
Warm waters. You should come.' I remember her
strong swim, in the North Atlantic waters off Cornwall.
How it almost ended. And here she is.

'That sounds divine. But I'm teaching in Hong Kong.'

'Teach in Thailand.' The words were out of my mouth
before I could think about them. Too much fruit juice.
Not enough beer, or we wouldn't be chatting at this
bar. This too-crowded bar.

But she's thinking about, and not immediately
rejecting, the idea.

'I suppose one classroom is the same as another.'

'Attagirl.'

She, rightly, rolls her eyes at me for that.

'Yeah, I'm still not convinced.' A spark of challenge in her eyes. That jut of her hips, her hands casually resting in the back of her jean's pocket.

'I'll buy your flight.'

She shakes her head.

'Too easy. We need the decision taken almost out of our hands'.

She glances around. I finish the rest of my drink, slamming the glass down a little too fiercely. Her attention focusses on the glass. On the bar. She turns, agonisingly slowly, the challenge now across her whole face.

'If I back flip across this bar, you can buy that flight.'

'What?' I shake my head. 'It sounded like you were going to back flip across this crowded room'.

'Not the room.' She taps the mahogany. 'The bar.'

She hops up on the edge, of, indeed, the bar, demonstrating the closest thing to lithely as I'd – hell, I'd never had cause to use that word before. Cheers rise around her. Staff stare, briefly, and she winks as she walks to the far end. Glasses are cleared.

I crane over people at the other end of the bar, to see her flex her arms, her fingers her hips, her legs, her feet. She grins over her shoulder at me and winks once more, before bending over backwards, into an inverted pose. Her arms easily reach the counter and hold on, as those gorgeously long legs sail into the air, amid more cheers. Her top rides up, exposing a hint of flesh.

Twice more she completes a somersault, until she sits, cross-legged on the bar opposite me, grinning. She takes a beer from some guy's hand, raises it to me and takes a sip. 'To Thailand.' She declares, hopping down to face me.

Drinks keep arriving, whether I was ordering them or Elle was, I couldn't tell. Customers came and went, and probably outside the night got darker then lighter. My head definitely felt heavier.

13

Elle

Mid-November

After his break, Jam returned to his kit.

He began a kick drum beat, and settled into an effortless performance of upbeat seventies rock that I really needed tonight.

He is mesmerising to watch, his bare arms and shoulders flexing in a, frankly, hypnotic way. His blue vest, worn with years of playing, knows the songs as well as he does.

One after another the instrumental songs burst forward. Other customers stood at the bar next to me have abandoned their drinks to watch, to listen. He doesn't need a guitar or vocalist to hold the room. A group of people join in on the chorus and I begin to feel more relaxed than I have done in months.

A quick half hour later he's off stage, to cheers and applause, and he heads straight for me. For the cocktails I'd ordered under his name.

He downs half and grins when I tell him he is incredible.

As a musician. Definitely.

'You should see Thailand, Elle. Crystal clear waters. Warm waters.'

Oh, to get out of this intense heat and sweat and noise and into the water.

But I can't afford to buy my own drinks. I am here until I can save to leave.

'That sounds divine. But I'm teaching in Hong Kong.'

'Teach in Thailand.'

I study his face. Sweet brown eyes that I know I can trust.

He is serious. He is also heading towards drunk.

Then he offers to buy my flight. Don't tease a girl, I think.

I couldn't take any money from him, but I could earn the opportunity. I wouldn't take charity. Not from Jam. If I asked he'd loan, but that would tilt us in a way I wasn't entirely comfortable with.

The sudden whack of glass against wood has me re-examining our surroundings. I look along the length of the bar, calculate its width, the drop. Easy; I'd worked with narrower.

'Back flip across this bar?' He repeats.

In answer I leap up on the wooden surface.

Glasses are moved, staff look up, but don't ask me to step down. The world is in alignment with my future. I walk the length of the bar, ascertaining risk, cheers rising from nearby. From the opposite end I see Jam crane his neck around to keep an eye on me. I stretch out my body, my arms, fingers, legs, toes. It's been a while, but the thousands of hours I spent in gymnastics is about to pay off.

In seconds I perform a triple back flip, back to Jam, and sit sipping a stranger's beer.

See, easy.

I can't wait to hit the waters of Thailand.

The next morning, I wake to my alarm invading my dreams.

I'm alone.

But I am going to Thailand.

I dress quickly, shoving all my belongings in my suitcase, and my travel essentials (laptop, Elemis beauty goodies, Mulberry travel wallet, Space NK silk sleep mask, which Zed bought me for my first Christmas in Boston, to remind me of the UK) into my day bag. I fill my small Macy's bag with leftover cereal bars, AKA lunch, and cookies and refill my water bottle.

Once I've checked out of the hotel, I stumble onto the corner of the street to catch the bus to take me to Jam's hotel. Fifteen minutes later I squeeze through the doors and walk the short distance to the building.

At the hotel's coffee shop I use the last of my money to buy an Americano and a latte, then take the elevator to Jam's floor; six, for the number of years we've known each other. Room number two.

My credit limit is maxed out and I've just won myself a one way flight to Thailand on a whim of work and no idea of salary. Maybe Jam would go on without me and I'd be in Hong Kong until further notice?

Shaking my head free of those unhelpful thoughts, I balance the cup holder in my left hand and rap on the door with my right. And wait, sweating under the weight of my bags, willing the door to open.

Eventually, the door pulls back to reveal much more than the room threshold I was expecting. I really wish he had more than a towel around his waist.

Or less, maybe.

I cross the line, 'Morning, gorgeous' I yell to his fragile state, handing him a cup as I march into the room. Stuff is everywhere. God, what if he's decided to stay in Hong Kong?

14
Jam

I was normally the one doing the pounding.

But there is definitely an external beat going on that is out of my control.

And it won't go away. I bury my head under the pillow, the feathers like bricks to my skull, hoping the neighbour's noise will soon subside.

Then I realise that part of the noise is in my head. The other beat, definitely out of time, is coming from ... the door? I hadn't pre-ordered room service, had I? I can't even speak.

But the knocking will only go away for one thing.

I fall out of bed and stumble to the door, grabbing a towel en route for modesty.

Elle stands before me, two coffee cups in her hand. She looks me up and down slowly, her eyes mischievous, even at this hour. She hands me a cup and crosses the threshold, I take the coffee, close the door with my butt and look around at the room carnage.

'Flight time, sunshine. We need to be at the airport in an hour. If we're still going to Thailand?'

I down half the coffee and nod to my discarded jeans and a vest from the back of the chair. Elle throws them over my arm and the coffee and I head into the bathroom. Elle sits down on the bed with her coffee, scanning the chaos in the room as I close the door.

In the shower, vague memories of last night, possibly early this morning, filter in with the piercing light. A bet among the shots last night. A travel app to book a flight in the early hours of the morning. Google Images of Thai beaches. A lot of glassware.

A bar.

Back flips across the bar.

Thailand.

Elle with a back pack and a suitcase; she's coming to Thailand with me.

A smile lifts one side of my mouth, before I wince at the sudden movement.

I emerge, only half-crappily, to a tidy room and a packed case, throw my empty cup in the bin.

'I got bored.' Elle offers, holding out a Danish for me. 'And called room service. You look like a man in need of pastry. You have a minute to double check the room and then we're off. I've never been to Thailand before. Will there be sharks?'

I nod and check the room. Everything has been tidied away, the bed stripped, ready for the cleaners. I finish the pastry and glance at Elle, stood by the door. Her eyes sparkle like the mid-afternoon Pacific and my head stops hurting.

On the street, I hold my hand out for a cab and one turns up quickly. I sling our bags in the trunk and climb in after Elle.

'What are you doing about your job here?' I ask.

'We came to a mutual agreement that I'm not the teacher they're looking for – I am definitely not my sister when it comes to imparting knowledge. I ask too many questions and they think I don't know anything. I explained there'd been an emergency and I had to leave Hong Kong – so they'd know I wasn't going to another employer on the island. But, don't worry - I can fake being happy in any job if it's near the beach.'

'I think you'll find the relaxed way of living, and teaching, is more suited to you. Large cities aren't for everyone. Boston isn't that big, especially if you're already part of a community, like you were at Harvard.'

'Hmmm, Boston.' She whispers, settling back into her seat as we head to the airport.

I had no idea what was about to happen.

15
Elle

I was in actual paradise.

The Andaman Sea was so warm it felt like I was in the pool of a five star spa facility. Except, no membership could compete with the natural beauty of nature. And the water was so crystal clear. I swam every morning before breakfast and every evening just before sunset. The pure white sandy beaches were nothing like I'd never seen before. I devoured gorgeous, fresh, chicken Pad Thai every day followed by pineapple smoothies. This was so far removed from the urban life I'd always known.

However, after only four weeks on the island, I know I'm not cut out to teach. Oh, everyone is so friendly – Thailand really is the land of smiles. But I have to be so attentive to others, and the early starts to the day are so different here. I worked hard at the gallery, but I didn't do any face-to-face communication until Fion rolled in.

And I have to be an entertainer as well as a teacher.

I have no idea how to teach a language I was born speaking. I don't know anything about grammatical structures, or all the stuff that is second-nature to Lucy. I seem to talk about a random topic they choose – like sandwiches, once they realised that the British Earl of

Sandwich was responsible for this western fast food, with lots of excited chatter about the perfect sandwich. But, I have no idea why anyone would want a soggy sandwich when you have fresh lime-flavoured noodles in minutes, with no plastic lunch box in sight.

There are three other western teachers here, too. Charlie is from Birmingham, so we argue regularly about the best city to live in the UK. It's Manchester, clearly. He's almost thirty and has been travelling and teaching his way around the world for the last five years, and has absolutely no plans to return to the UK.

Alex, a couple of years older than me, from northern California, is an absolute adventurer and fearless when it comes to hiking and camping, and she has so much energy, without even the aid of caffeine. I thought I was active, but I'm sedentary compared to her four am yoga starts.

Then there's Tomas from Denmark, who is a primary school teacher over here on a professional placement until February. He's lovely, although keeps to himself mainly, spending his evenings preparing for the next day and video chatting with his wife, who's working on her PhD in Copenhagen.

I share a one room beach hut apartment with Alex. Jam shares a hut with Charlie. Tomas has an apartment to himself, as the professional, who needed more space to prepare lessons and write his reports for home.

Now it was the end of my first month here. And my first pay day. It felt good to earn again, and the prices being low meant I could actually save for my own return flight when the time came. Although I wasn't in a hurry to leave paradise.

'Wotcha, Elle.' Charlie greets me with a hug, pours a beer for me from the jug on the table.

'Hey Charlie, what a week, eh?'

I forgot how much I missed this small talk from a fellow Brit. Mindless and connecting at the same time.

'Alex is on her way back from diving'.

'I really need to sort out my Padi qualification when I'm out here.'

'I can take you diving. Any time. If you like going down.'

'Oh, God, Charlie, that's terrible.' I laugh, raising a drink to his awful innuendo.

I search around the bar. People of various ages and nationalities relax, enjoying another night in heaven.

Jam sits on a chair next to me, drumsticks raring to go.

'You playing later, man?' Charlie asks. Jam nods, grinning, an internal beat taking over his whole body, from his head, rippling through his arms, to his tanned legs displaying a light coating of hair lightened from the sun.

'How was your day, Elle?' He asks, swinging his head and shoulders into a rhythm.

'How can I complain? Stunning surroundings, delicious lunches, and the children here are very sweet, even if they are so chatty when learning. Plus, it's pay day.'

'You can buy me a free beer later.'

'Anytime.' I raise my glass again, as Tomas walks over, collapsing into a chair. More beer arrives, from the twenty-something Thai girl sweeping her long, straight black hair behind her as she studies our party. I've never been able to grow my hair longer than my shoulder before it drove me crazy and I was cropping it short again. Maybe one day I'd wear extensions, just to feel how different long hair would be, properly long, like this woman's mane.

Alex walked in a few minutes later, fresh with stories of under the sea. We ordered dinner and afterwards Jam took to the drum kit. His Friday night complete, I thought, as I watched him try to resolve a barely-contained energy.

We drank and danced and ate our way towards Saturday. Just before dawn someone suggested we go swimming. Jam tore into the sea, his back silhouetted in the early light as he spread out his limbs, no doubt aching from hours of drumming. Charlie splashed ahead, carving up the still ocean. I slowly waded into the shallow depths. The water was even more welcome now, after a month of treading water, financially speaking. I hadn't had to be careful with money since I'd gone to the US, thanks to my scholarship, my part-time job and my social connections.

I floated on my back, looking up at the fading night sky. I felt something brush past my arm and sprang forward, thinking only of sharks and breakfast. My heart raced from the fast swim I prepared for, at the same time as the shark laughed. I turned to face Jam's brown eyes smirking at me.

I shoved water in his face in childish retaliation, and of course he mirrored my action.

But the thought of sharks looking for human croissants had me swimming to the shoreline. My long-haired shark swam alongside me.

We sat on the sand, drying off, as the sun rose ahead of us.

'I never got to thank you.' I said.

Jam turned towards me, puzzled.

'Back in Boston, at the gallery event. On the phone.'

'Oh, sure. It's what family does – looks out for each other.'

'That has to be one of the worst nights I've ever experienced.' I shuddered, and Jam scooched closer, droplets of water sliding down his arms and soaking the sand.

'What did happen that night?'

'Oh, you know, I spectacularly embarrassed my boss, lost my future.'

'Your future?'

I nodded. 'To own a gallery by the sea.' But the memory was still too fresh for me to talk about. No gallery wanted to know me now. 'Come on, race you to breakfast.'

I took off across the beach towards our small group of huts, to shower. Jam must have taken a short cut, as I met him outside his hut seconds later.

'Draw?' I declared, yawning. He nodded, and we agreed to meet in a few minutes for pancakes.

I stepped into the bathroom, already steamy from Alex's use, and ran the cool water. My thirty minute shower was down to just five minutes. I simply didn't have the access, or the funds, to the shelves of products I had used in Boston. There was no point spending ages in the bathroom when I swam a couple of times a day. I washed my hair every morning in coconut shampoo, letting it dry in the sun, and used just one shower gel, also coconut-scented. Once a week I left coconut conditioner on my hair, the black now almost faded out, with my dark brown hair finding the light. The sea and the sand were my natural exfoliator and body polish. Sun cream had become my new moisturiser.

Jam and I met outside our huts a few minutes later and walked towards the centre of the island. I was looking forward to catching up on sleep for most of the day. At the restaurant, Alex was already finishing up her granola, a day bag by her feet.

'You off somewhere else to sleep?' I asked, pulling out a stool to sit on.

She nodded, sipping her green smoothie.

'Going out on a boat to a nearby island – wanna come?'

'Ah, I promised Don, that I'd help him learn about football teams in England later.'

'I'll go on the boat with you.' Jam said. And something sank into my stomach as I saw Alex's face light up.

Bloody football and promises.

Breakfast arrived quickly and Jam ate as fast as I'd ever seen him. I watched them both walk towards the harbour, staring until they'd climbed onto the boat.

I picked up my iced coffee and headed back to the hut, passing out as soon as I pulled the mosquito netting around me.

When I woke Alex still wasn't back. I hunted around for a bag of team badges I'd bought online, and went in search of Don.

He was outside my front door, playing with a stick, when I stepped outside. His smile was infectious and my mood quickly lifted. After a discussion about whether City or United were the best team, I reminded him that I had spent the last few years in America, and that I actually preferred hockey. We went through all the teams he knew, practising his vocabulary and geographic knowledge of the UK, and he proudly pinned the badges to his white shirt.

I'd already arranged to go to Don's house for dinner, with his sister, Malee. The all-nighter was beginning to have an impact. But a promise was a promise, and I knew she was a close friend of Jam's. I wasn't about to embarrass him or me. I'd learned that much from networking.

I'd been over for dinner a couple of times with Jam, and I liked Malee. Like her younger brother, her smile was infectious. She worked hard, seemingly at restaurants, guest houses and markets across the island. There didn't seem to be any other family. She treated Jam like her younger brother, and I could sense a connection, a respect, between them. She was a fascinating person to listen to, full of wisdom and prayer and a belief that she was only one part of an infinite picture. I'd always come away with a peaceful mind after a visit to her house.

Malee was near the counter top stove in their apartment when we returned, stirring something in a pan. I was told to use the bathroom first, and then Don would.

Malee set the dishes of steaming bowls, fragrant with lime and coconut, at their table outside the apartment, and I helped with drinks. After a short prayer of thanks, heads bowed, hands clasped, we tucked into the delicious food. A lifetime of eating in Manchester and Boston's best restaurants doesn't compare with the delicate flavours of authentic Thai food. I was learning that there was an underlying calm to all movements, and a sense of enjoying being in every moment.

I forgot about my lack of sleep, and I'd almost forgotten about Alex and Jam, until they came sauntering past in the evening sun, wet from a swim. My eyes watched them walk past, deep in conversation. Jam nodded at us and I managed a brief smile.

'You like James.' Malee said.

'What? Of course – he's like family.'

'Sure. Family.' She said, in a way that made me think of something more than family.

But speaking of family, I ought to check in with Lucy soon, it had been so long since we'd talked and I missed her. I said my goodbyes walked across the quiet island to the huts.

Back in my hut I sent Lucy a quick message to find out if she was free for a Skype chat. She video-called back immediately, and I realised it was just breakfast time in Nashville. Thankfully, Lottie was an early riser.

We caught up, and I said hello to my scrumptious niece. Lucy looked huge, but assured me it was all water, and she was looking forward to welcoming her new baby in a few months.

'So, Thailand?' She asked.

'Er, yep, an opportunity came up.'

'And Jam was that opportunity.'

'What?'

'You look well.' She always could distract me.

'Well, I'm swimming every day, wandering around in lots of sunlight, and the food is incredible. I'm sorry I won't be with you at Christmas, though.' We both paused, lost in what the festive season would mean for us this year.

'I know. But we'll have another Christmas when you next come out here.' I caught the tail end of something in her voice and sat up.

'Everything okay, Lucy?'

'Hmm-hmmm.' I waited. 'Oh, these hormones are playing havoc. I'm probably horrible to live with.'

'Lucy.'

She started crying then and I just listened, wishing I could hug her and tell her everything was okay. I tried not to cry myself.

'Oh, Elle. I know Cain works hard, he's doing everything he can so we can have time as a family when the baby arrives.'

'But.'

'But he keeps getting these messages that he sort of grimaces at and he sinks his shoulders. When I ask him what's wrong he says it's nothing.'

'But you think it is.'

'I'm still so new to all this. Raising a family. Being in love with a gorgeous man. God, I sound awful.'

'Not at all, Luce. It's not you talking, but your baby and instincts and hormones. Do I sound like I know what I'm talking about?'

'Yup.' She laughed. 'It's so good to talk to you. Oh, there's someone at the door – Cain has a full house of people on their way....take care out there, tell Jam I said hi. I love you.'

'Love you, too, Sis. Give Lottie and my brother-in-law a squish from me!'

I threw the phone down on the bed and sighed.

I had to keep teaching until I earned the money to go back to the States. Though, I didn't know what I'd be going back to. And Boston was cold in December. If I could last here until spring, maybe I'd have found another job in a gallery where Fion hadn't blacklisted me.

I updated my socials, with a few photos of Thailand, and AJ posted a double thumbs-up. Man of few words for a writer.

I closed down my phone and got ready for bed.

Just as I was drifting off, I saw the scurrying of legs on the wall. I switched on my lamp and spotted a humdinger of a spider looking at me, inches away from my bed.

'Hello, sunshine', I declared, keeping my eyes on him, sliding out from under the net and looking for something to help me relocate him. I reached for a bowl, placing it quickly over the spider, moving just a little faster than him. I slid a Manila folder underneath the bowl and escorted him outside.

Charlie and Tomas were chatting over beers at a table outside Charlie's hut, and their conversation stopped when they saw me. I nodded hello, as I returned Sammy to nature.

Back in the room I remembered the t-shirt I slept in didn't leave anything to the imagination. Never mind, it covered more than my swimsuit.

I settled back down to sleep.

16
Jam

Christmas Day

We taught right up until Christmas Eve and Christmas Day was crazier than it had ever been.

Only twelve more hours to endure.

This year I was grateful for distractions from the others. I knew the day was coming, the inevitable could not be avoided, but the run up had been easier this year, with the expats. We had never had such a wide community. Elle was great at organising us all, even if it was just dinner together. People migrated towards her and a table was never empty if she could help it.

She'd even managed to arrange a Santa visit for the children, thanks to online shopping and a wiling Charlie, and presents were exchanged. Don never left her side, his eyes focused always on her. Quite possibly he was in a bit of a crush. Elle always had time for him, and his Aunt, Malee, the people I returned to each year.

After dinner tonight, board games were found, and I teamed up with a de-Santa'd Charlie, against Elle and Alex; we won Monopoly, but they won Scrabble.

We all drank a little too much.

'Truth or dare time.' Charlie declared, once the children had returned home, laden with presents.

Elle and Alex sat forward, clearly used to this game. I sipped my beer hoping it'd be a quick round. I was starting to get antsy. I always did.

'I am in.' Tomas said, and I raised my beer to him.

Charlie twisted the empty beer bottle and we all watched it spin around the table. It landed on Alex.

'Dare.' She laughed.

'Arm wrestle.' Charlie demanded, clearing the space. He easily won, as Alex kept laughing.

She spun the bottle and it landed opposite Tomas.

'Truth.'

'Do you like teaching?' Alex asked.

'Of course, this is my career. This is all I have ever wanted to do.'

The bottle landed at Elle. I knew the dares she was capable of.

'Truth.' She eventually decided. A little part of me was disappointed.

'What's the most romantic thing anyone has ever done for you?' Alex asked.

Elle paused, her gaze shifting. Probably as she sifted through memories.

'I've had plenty of dinner dates.' She eventually said.

'Yeah, but romantic?'

I could see her struggling and all eyes were on her.

'I bet you couldn't beat me in a race to the bar. Backwards.' I stood, and placed my bottle down. Would she? She was out of her seat before I'd finished my thought out loud, lining up next to me.

'Count us down, Tomas.' She said and when the one landed in the night air, we tore backwards to the bar, giggling, side by side.

'Thanks for the distraction, Jam.' She whispered, as we hit the wooden door frame, then turned and ran forwards to the rejoin the others.

The bottle eventually spun on me. 'Truth' I agreed, reluctantly. I was starting to need my space.

'How many times have you been to Thailand?' Elle asked.

'For more than half my life.' I answered, before I had chance to think. Or retract.

'Wow, you really like the Thai ... food, man.' Charlie laughed.

'Ah, okay, I'm calling it a night. Merry Christmas, everyone.' I stood, smiling, finishing the last of my beer.

I tried to shake off Elle's questioning stare as I ambled back to the hut.

17

Elle

Boxing Day

I returned to my hut, shortly after Jam left. He must have gone straight inside and hit the lights as it was already dark in his place. He'd been quiet for the last few days and that admission of spending so many years in Thailand? What was the pull?

I opened the door and felt the cool of the tiles under my feet as I walked to the bathroom for a shower before bed.

I couldn't remember when a Christmas Day had been so busy, or more enjoyable. In the UK I'd traditionally stayed with friends for most of the day. Mum and Dad weren't big on parenting, so December 25th had just been another day to them.

My friends' families had always included me and we exchanged gifts. But there was always a part of me missing; they had years of memories to share. Elle had visited for my final year in the UK, and that's when I'd learned that not only did she know Cain Adams, but he was very much in love with her.

I started the shower and stood under the cooling spray, using up the last of my gorgeous travel-sized Clarins body wash, which I kept for when my senses needed a little something extra. The aroma of summer time gardens lifted my lips into a smile.

In Boston, Christmas had also been quiet. Lucy and Cain usually always went to Cornwall. I didn't take time away from the gallery, so usually on the actual day I was in my room studying, devouring all the British snacks I'd scored on the run up – the last of my Cadbury's advent calendar that Nancy and Joe had sent me, a massive packet of Burt's Sea Salt crisps, a huge tray of Ferrero Rocher hazelnut chocolates, all yummy treats that Lucy arranged for Nancy to post out to me. One Christmas they'd even planned to come to Boston, but I just said I couldn't take time off.

I switched off the shower and wrapped myself in the pink DKNY towel I'd refused to let go of. I smiled each time I saw the now-worn cotton fabric, remembering my shopping days in Boston, when Zed and I would pour over the home items, decorating our rooms. Everything else had been sold, but this towel would travel with me.

I wasn't tired tonight, though, and there was no sign of Alex to chat with. I slipped into my night shirt and took my laptop to bed. I uploaded my photos of the day to my social pages, and then roamed around online. Suddenly, a news item caught my eye and I sat up, scrolling through pages and pages of Boxing Day memories online, and school fundraisers in my mind. When I couldn't read any more I closed the laptop and curled up, but I couldn't sleep.

There was no sound of movement outside, just the gentle waves lapping the shore.

I couldn't imagine what this island paradise must have been like all those years ago as waves as big as buildings crashed down, destroying everything, taking thousands of lives.

Claiming Jam's family.

As dawn breaks I climb out of bed and dress. Jam and I normally swim before breakfast, but I can't see him in the water and he's not lurking outside waiting for me. Through his hut window I can see his bed is made, and Charlie is sprawled across his cover, net hanging open; he's going to have a few new bites later. I walk away from the beach towards the north.

The island has a peak with stunning views of the landscape below. It takes me just under an hour to reach the top. I stop to rest, looking out across the early morning sea.

The terror and the devastation the Tsunami caused to this beautiful island, and the communities along the Indian Ocean, occupies my thoughts. Two hundred and twenty seven thousand lives lost. How many people on this island lost family? How can you recover, wondering if the same would ever happen again?

Blotting away tears with my fists, I turn away from the turquoise blue backdrop and reach the summit.

Ahead, I finally see Jam. He's staring out across the water, looking for the entire world like he wants solitude.

He shouldn't be alone.

I step towards him, my tread slow and deliberate on the stony ground.

He doesn't look my way until I'm right behind him.

Then he briefly smiles and turns his gaze back towards the water.

I move closer.

'You were here in 2004, weren't you?' I whisper. 'This happened to your family, didn't it?'

His simple nod tears that organ I thought was impenetrable; my heart. I wrap my arms around his chest, resting my cheek against his back. Out of somewhere come the words I've heard from Malee. I hesitate over the prayer, reliant on memory, and Jam joins in, gripping my arms.

'With every breath I take today,
I vow to be awake;
And every step I take,
I vow to take with a grateful heart.
So I may see with eyes of love
Into the hearts of all I meet,
To ease their burden when I can
And touch them with a smile of peace'.

His grip tightens.

'James Logan, you lost everything that day, but you are twice most men I know. Your parents are so proud of you.' He turns around, nuzzles into my neck, his arms wrapped around my back. I easily support his weight, and I realise the silence between us is the longest we've ever been quiet together.

And I could stay like this forever.

'Your Mum thinks your hair is too long though, and your Dad wonders when you'll get a proper job, even though you travel the world.' My words dissolve into his laughter, and he throws his head back in physical enjoyment. Or release. I'm not sure which.

'I'm glad you're here, Elle.' He rasps, his hands loose around my waist.

I nod, the rising sun glinting in my eyes, making them water. I hold him close, my hands stroking his back, his head resting on my shoulder.

'Last one down buys the iced coffee.' I whisper, turning away from his embrace to scramble down the path.

I don't need to look back to know he will follow. I hear his footsteps, and I quicken my pace, taking wide corners of the spiral path, to keep my advantage.

I would have won, too, had he not used his unfairly sized arms to reach past me and pull me to one side, as the path entered the open space.

Laughing, panting, we agreed to buy each other coffee.

At the restaurant, Don approaches, wielding his collection of football badges, earned from me and gifted from Santa. He talks a mile a minute, and is the right kind of distraction from the silent reverie Jam and I have fallen into.

Jam chats easily with him about sport, and I sip the rest of my coffee, raising my hand to order another one. My lack of sleep is catching up with me but I'm reluctant to leave just yet.

18

Jam

Boxing Day

I'd been coming to Thailand for longer than I'd lost my family.

But, for the early morning moment on Boxing Day, when I climbed to the top of the viewpoint for reflection, I'd always been alone.

I inhaled Elle's coconut scent, offered a small smile when I saw her, before turning to be alone with my thoughts.

Then I felt her arms around my chest, the warmth of her cheek pressed against my back.

I was immobile. How had she known? I knew Cain wouldn't have said anything.

Her voice, wandering over words I'd said a thousand times.

Peace.

Had I found something close to it?

My voice blended with hers, to finish the prayer, my body growing hot where her arms remained, my fingers clung to her.

And then she said the words I'd thought so many times alone. That I make them proud. Not past tense. Present.

Mum can see us now, I know, her book put to one side as she watches her boy unravel from the inside.

And she would suggest a hair cut! And Dad would rib me about being a drummer instead of a guitarist.

No woman had ever been so close to me that they understood me from the inside.

I was lost all over again.

I loved Elle.

I was as certain, as calm and as terrified as I'd ever been.

When she challenged me to a race back down to the shore, it was just what I'd needed.

I couldn't tell her how I felt.

Yet.

I was happy to jog behind her, catching her arm at the last moment and turning her around, so that I easily won. Her skin warm, her eyes sparkling, caught up, and in ...something.

Whether she felt it or not, our relationship had just changed.

19

Elle

Every morning Jam and I coordinated our swim times, meeting just as the sun rose, warming up our limbs quietly and spending half an hour in the water before half an hour's quiet chat on the sand. I learned about his Mum's love for music, how it drew his Dad to her. How they'd taught him kindness and respect and following your own path, a belief that his Uncle Eddie, who he'd gone to live with, had upheld. He regaled me with tales of gigging around California, developing a musical knowledge no classroom could provide. When I'd been his age I was studying and working two jobs to make sure I could leave the life I was born into. But it had been my purpose, my choice. How would it have been had the decision been taken from me?

Jam shared how he made peace with the country that took his parents from him, returning first with his Uncle for a couple of years, who wanted him to trust the ocean, before returning to connect with the island in his own ways, sharing his love of music with anyone who would listen.

He told me how he'd met a kindred soul of music and the ocean in Cain; the brother he never had, who helped him through grief over the loss of his Aunt, and trying to find his way in Nashville.

I told him I sometimes missed England, but not enough to return there, as Lucy was living in Nashville – which she would be forever. I wasn't ready to return to a Boston winter, and didn't know what I'd do there. He told me how I was always welcome to use his house in Newquay if I needed fish and chips and tea and the cold ocean.

Then we'd go back to our huts and prepare for our teaching days, before repeating the routine of swim and drying on the sand in the evening.

We'd taught a few classes after the New Year celebrations, but I struggled to concentrate in the heat. My already waning enthusiasm for being in a class of enthusiastic young children was really stretching my mind and my resources.

I spent afternoons napping and catching up online with Zed and Lucy. Tim and Jake were working on new projects, and Fion still hadn't updated the gallery page since I'd last worked on it, although local news sites shared details of regular showings. More discreet, membership-only, affairs. It seemed like everyone else was moving on, doing something, in the New Year. I was alternating sweating with swimming.

One afternoon, Alex and I were sat at a table near the beach, under the shade of a palm tree, sipping our fast-melting smoothies.

'Don't you think Jam is hot?' She asked, twirling the straw in her green concoction. 'I would kill for an afternoon on a boat with him, my legs wrapped around his waist.'

'Bloody hell, Alex, give a girl a warning, eh?' I laughed, trying not to choke on pineapple pieces. Then I pictured her suggestion and I felt myself flush.

'Or even Charlie, you know. If you can spare him.'

'Spare him?' I repeated, draining my smoothie and tilting my head.

'You know he has a thing for you, right?'

'Oh, that's just because we're both British.' I reasoned. I had absolutely no interest in Charlie.

'You mean you wouldn't?' Alex asked, sitting forward.

'Nope. His talking would be too distracting.'

Alex laughed, then, 'Yeah, Jam would concentrate the mind more.'

'I would, why?' Jam strolled towards the table, pulling up a chair to join us. I hid my face from Jam so he couldn't see my blush, while Alex fell about. She was no help. I ran my tongue over my teeth, took a deep breath and lied to Jam for the first time.

'We were talking about films.' I supplied. 'You have some great recommendations.' Alex fell about again, and I stood to say goodbye, the lure of an afternoon swim calling me, feeling suddenly hotter than usual. I didn't want to think about what Alex was thinking.

'Elle, wait up.' Jam strode into step beside me. 'I came to ask if you wanted to go for a swim.'

'I was just about to change into my cossie.' I blurted out, too late to back out.

'Cool, see you in a few minutes.' Jam jogged backwards towards his apartment, and I felt my axis tilt a little. I couldn't afford to screw things up between us. He was one of the family.

And I didn't think I could be rejected by him again.

My swim was all off. I didn't like high sun swims – mornings or evenings were much cooler. Jam kept hovering, too, and all I could think about were his legs, which kept brushing against mine. I'd never needed to quench a thirst so much.

'I'm heading back,' I said. 'Headache starting.'

'You okay? I'll come with you.'

I put my hand on his chest to stop him. Felt the heat on my palm, even through the ocean. But I couldn't pull away.

'No, no, it's okay, you stay here. I'll be fine. Just probably need a lie down.' Oh the images that sprang forward. I turned away and swam to the shore. Each time I glanced back I saw Jam watching me. His concerns were sweet. I waved as I reached the sand, and watched him swim out further to sea.

20

Jam

Mid January

I met Elle coming out of her apartment for her morning swim, just like she did every day. Except it was a little later as it was Saturday, so we didn't have to be in a classroom for eight o'clock. I knew she was losing interest in teaching.

'Morning.' I called out and she smiled in greeting as she stretched one arm across the other. She was the first to throw down the physical challenge today, and as she called out one I followed her lead to the sea, feeling at home when the water hit my body and I could submerge in the beautiful waters.

Around us, traditional Thai boats returned from their fishing trips, were being unpacked. Birds circled ahead and sea creatures darted around and between us. As Elle's pace slowed I joined her, treading water. She looked utterly at peace in the water, like she was made to be here.

'What are you thinking about?' I asked.

'Boston.' Her swift reply. Her city. Her life.

'Do you miss it?' Home sickness was a common thing after a few months into a new routine, when excitement and adrenalin were in a dip.

I was surprised at her reply of no. But then, there was no daily swim opportunity in Boston's harbour.

I turned back to the sand, my body gliding through the water, committed to showing Elle the simple pleasures that non-Boston life offered.

As she exited the water, slicking her hair back from her face, I fell into step beside her.

'Pancakes on me, to counteract the home sickness? And as a bribe?'

She glanced sideways at me. 'What's on your mind, Logan?'

Her use of my surname unlocked something inside me. 'Help me, Elle. Help me teach.'

Her eyes widened and she bumped into my upper arm with hers, then shot away at the electric shock.

'Teaching. On a Saturday. Going to need a large coffee with breaky, Logan.'

She nodded and smiled her incredible smile and I stood watching her memory, long after she had retrieved her key and entered her hut.

Malee brought our breakfasts and Elle's coffee out to us, and I tucked into the double pancakes, devouring them without conversation, giving her time to think about the chance to teach together this morning.

Don was excited to learn a new western song, I'd explained, and his friends, although they were reluctant sometimes to learn English, would only benefit from Don's energy for learning. I wanted to teach Don not just a song, but a song that I hoped would give him perspective. He was about to grow up to be the man of the family, looking after his Aunty, and I knew from experience how music could teach more than just lyrics. Uncle Eddie absolutely loved The Beach Boys, so I'd chosen a simple song to get us started.

After breakfast we walked to the music room, where I was due to meet the kids.

Elle seemed lost in her thoughts as she finished her coffee. I was desperate to know what she was thinking, suddenly wishing I was that vampire who could read minds. Had I selfishly upturned her day?

Don and his friends were already waiting, and the room was suddenly filled with noise and shouts of Mr Jam. When they saw Elle they calmed a little, but Elle said I was their teacher today, and she retreated quietly to a desk, watching us all carefully, a soft smile on her face. The boisterousness resumed.

I quickly tuned a guitar and started playing the classic sixties song, *When I Grow Up to Be a Man*. The boys swayed, and recognised the numbers in the backing vocals. I wrote some lyrics on the board, wishing I'd brought handouts with me.

Elle moved to the chalk board and erased my scrawl, suggesting that the song may not be completely understood otherwise, then rewrote the words. She had beautiful handwriting, and I forced myself away from watching her, retuning the guitar instead. I asked for a volunteer to sing the main part and Don was thrust forward. I gave the others some *chap lek* cymbals to strike when I gave the nod.

Over the next couple of hours, Don swapped position and they all took a turn with the instruments and leading the vocals. But they were sounding good. We had a discussion about growing up, and responsibilities, which the boys seemed to already understand. They asked me about America, and I told them I had grown up in the same state as The Beach Boys music, which led to talk of surfing and listening to a lot of live music.

The sound of stomachs rumbling halted the lesson, and the boys ran off for lunch and to run around with a soccer ball afterwards.

'I've never heard you sing lead before. You should do that more often.'

I grinned, feeling as childish as the song we'd just spent the afternoon with. My fingers played with the strings. 'What do you listen to, Elle?'

'Go loud or go home...has to be rock. Sorry, country boy.' She smiled.

I found the chords for a Springsteen song, *Tougher than the Rest*.

'Springsteen is good, but how about the Foos?'

I switch up the tempo and open up a Foo Fighter medley, starting with *All My Life*, via *Monkey Wrench* and *Learn to Fly*. I end with the ballad *Times Like These* and looked up at Elle. Her chin rested on knuckles. I've never seen her so silent.

I could play songs just for her my whole damn life.

'You have a fantastic inner Grohl.' She eventually said. 'You should teach a Foos song to Don, and teach him the drums.'

'Not a bad idea. Malee might not be impressed.'

'Malee.' Elle echoed her name again. 'She was on the island that day, too, wasn't she?'

I nodded, continuing to strum as I watched the connection form in her eyes. 'Mum, Dad, me, we were all safe. When the Tsunami hit we'd been walking near the peak. Could see the waves. And just ran up. We told everyone we saw to climb high. Malee was sat on a rock, refusing to move, kept saying her sister was at the beach. Dad tried to encourage her to move. Finally, Mum said if Malee took me up, they'd go back for her sister. They asked me to take care of her. Wrapped me in their arms, told me they loved me.'

'Oh, fuck, James.'

'No one returned. Emergency services brought us down, just before night. Malee didn't leave my side. When Uncle Eddie came, a few days later, I begged him to take Malee, but she didn't want to leave the island.'

I stopped playing.

'I owe my life to Malee. If I hadn't had to stay with her, I'd have followed my parents.'

Elle stands up to hug me, her arms wrapped around my neck. When she pulls away, her scent lingers. She wipes her eyes with the palms of her hands.

'Hey. It's okay.' I utter, torn between wanting to comfort her and to never let go. I'm glad my guitar is still between us. 'I made my peace with nature a long time ago. What happened, happened, and no amount of wishing and hoping is going to change that. But this is why I return to Thailand each year. I'm glad you're here.'

'Me too, Jam, me too.'

I play When I Grow up again, my fingers grazing the strings over and over again, until Elle starts requesting other songs, no longer sad as the choices become more obscure, challenging me as the afternoon wears on, her eyes sharp and her voice sweet as she accepts defeat and on the same breath throws up another lyric for me to play.

We eventually pack up and walk back to the huts, our limbs side by side, colliding more than once.

'Dinner?' I ask.

'Always. See you in five.'

I knew I didn't have to keep inviting Elle to meals, but I guess a part of me wanted to look after her. I'd spent a long time looking after Lucy's sister, whether at gigs or in work, or, almost fatally, in the ocean. Now, I simply wanted her to enjoy as many gorgeous Thai meals as she could, while she could. She still preferred the lime and nut flavours of a Pad Thai above the livelier red or green curries, even if they were flavoured with coconut, a fragrance she wore so well.

Our meal was interrupted by the arrival of the other western teachers. Alex and Tomas, red-faced and fresh from their boat trip, Charlie from whatever endeavour he'd been up to, and some other western holiday makers, from the East coast and happy to hear travel tips from western locals.

Malee places another beer in front of me, and I asked for an iced coffee for Elle; like Lucy, she's the only person I know who isn't affected by drinking coffee before bed.

Suddenly, Charlie upends his beer across Elle. I watch as he immediately sinks down to her lap, a half-assed attempt at clearing the beer with the use of his shirt, rubbing the cotton against Elle's legs. She brushes him away, and he wanders off.

Tomas appears with a cloth, which Elle uses to wipe herself down. I was grateful she didn't call it a night. I move my chair around to sit between her and Tomas. The conversation inevitably turns to films, sparked by a movie Tomas has seen in Thailand. I've spent so long with Lucy and Cain that I'm definitely more knowledgeable about films than I ever have been. It's amazing what I'd picked up from focussing on the screen and not their content, entwined bodies on the couch.

I'd been aware that Charlie had been gone for a while, and a few moments later Elle stands and heads in the same direction as her fellow Brit. Tomas is in full throttle enthusing about the career of Leonardo DiCaprio so I'm unable to move away without seeming rude. I couldn't very well spend the day teaching others how to behave in society, and then run off mid-conversation. But no part of me was comfortable until I knew Elle was settled into her hut each night. Thailand wasn't always a safe place after hours - too much nature and too much dark.

As Tomas moves his bottle to his mouth, I stand and nod goodnight, heading in the same direction as Elle.

I find them both by the water's edge. Arms wrapped together. Intimately.

Then Elle's knee raises, nudging Charlie backwards; she steadies herself amongst the rocks.

I move towards them, reaching out for Elle at the same time as she steps back and away from Charlie. My hands land on his back instead, as he doubles-over vomiting.

'Time to head back, Charlie-boy.' I call out, steering him away from Elle.

I hear the familiar sound of Elle's walk as she follows us back to the accommodation, and I mouth good night as I watch her enter her room.

This was not how I'd hoped the night would end.

21

Elle

Mid-January

I stretch out along my bed, enjoying the very Saturday feel about the day. My body has gotten used to the early morning swim and classroom starts.

I check my phone for the time - a few minutes before eight. A little while longer and then I'll put on my swimsuit and enjoy the water before it becomes too hot. I stretch again, the thin covers light on my skin, the mosquito gauze moving as I move. I could almost be in a four poster bed, surrounded by romantic drapes.

I glance across at the empty bed.

Looks like Alex didn't come home again last night.

I snort and climb out of bed, changing into my one piece swim suit. I lock up and put the key under a nearby stone.

Even after living here for almost two months I'm still stunned by the turquoise water and white sand.

'Morning.' Jam approaches from the left and I smile in greeting as we synch our warm ups.

'Three, two, one.' I declare, running into the surf until my knees are wet, then swimming out into the sea. Jam isn't far behind. There are a few other swimmers out, but we are the only western teachers. After a little while we find ourselves treading water together, arms lazily drawing circles around us.

'Is it almost time for pancakes?' Jam asks.

'Soon. I love being in the sea.' I close my eyes.

I never thought I'd put swimming above caffeine. In Boston my Saturday would have begun with a coffee shop visit. And depending on how Saturday night went, possibly Sunday, too.

'What are you thinking about?'

'Boston.'

'Do you miss it?'

I open my eyes, preparing to swim off.

'Not at the moment.' I answer, swimming under the water back to the shore. Jam is already on the sand when I climb out.

'Pancakes on me to counteract the home sickness?' He asks. 'And as a bribe?'

I can't believe I'll be with the kids on a Saturday. But his puppy-dog brown eyes could flail an assassin.

In the hut, Alex is sat on her bed, hair and body wrapped in towels, earphones in.

'Morning.' I shout, and she waves back at me as she continues to apply her make-up.

My shower is brief, the almost-smell of pancakes motivating, and I quickly dry myself off before stepping into a red wrap around skirt and blue t-shirt. I still can't get used to the feeling of plastic seating on my bare legs when I wear shorts.

'Coming out for breakfast?' I ask Alex, and she removes her earphone.

'What? Oh, no thanks, I'm heading out with Tomas on a boat trip.'

'No worries – enjoy yourselves.'

'We will, we will', she cackles, as I close the door.

Jam is leaning on the side of a building as I head towards the bar, and falls into step beside me.

We arrive at our favourite restaurant, run by Malee. She places the usual in front of us. Chocolate, banana and three pancakes for me, double for Jam, with cream. Extra large coffee for me.

At the school Jam picks up a guitar from the music room, and some Thai instruments. Don is waiting with five of his friends when we arrive in the classroom at ten

Jam high-fives everyone, and I sit nearby, on a table, and listen to the boys chatter along to Jam about football. They had long ago realised I know nothing about the Premiership and although I grew up near Manchester, that was where my usefulness had ended. They were all unfailingly polite to me as their teacher, still, but the banter was for knowledgeable-about-everything Jam and his musical skills.

'Teach us. Mr Jam.' Don states, the leader of the group.

'I have an incredible song for you to learn today. A classic song from the 1960s.'

'Too old.' One of the boys moans, earning a friendly whack from Don, and a wise expression from Jam.

'Without history we are no one. Every musician needs to know their past to create their future.' He sounds like a grammatically correct Yoda.

'Yes, Mr Jam. We will listen to you.' Don declares, frowning at his friend, who is now at the back of the group.

Jam moves position slightly, so that he is in the centre of all the boys, and no one is left out. He tunes up the guitar, the instruments on a desk in front of the boys.

We all lean forward in anticipation.

The opening bars sound familiar, then the line, *'When I grow up to be a man.'*
Jam plays the rest of The Beach Boys' song, gauging the reaction of the boys. They hang on Jam's every move, and listen intently to the lyrics.

Jam writes the simple lyrics in wide scrawl on the board, and that's when I take the chalk from him, realising my purpose is so that the boys can actually read what is written.

I erase his scrawl and begin again, thankful Jam hasn't chosen a more complicated song.

Within the hour the boys are finger-snapping, playing instruments and harmonising along to the song. Already they look like the men they would grow into. No doubt inspired by a long-haired, surf-mad music teacher from America.

I realise this is the first time I've seen Jam away from his drum kit, and the first time I've heard him sing. I hadn't given his talent much credit, but Cain should definitely use his skills more.

The lesson ends and the boys run off for lunch, and to play football, no doubt.

Neither Jam or I move.

He plays a Springsteen song I'm vaguely familiar with, but I live in the twenty-first century. I ask if he knows anything by the Foos and four incredible tracks later I am aware of my thinly-disguised awe and shock.

I could listen to this man play all night. I could even listen to country music sung this way.

I don't know what makes me think of the connection, but I work out that Don and Malee are the reason that Jam keeps returning to the island. Don is too young to have been in the Tsunami, but Malee?

Jam nods, and tells me more about the Boxing Day tsunami. I picture their fear as they run to the top of the peak. Seeing Malee, trying to get her to move.

The agonising decision to ask Malee and Jam, children of ten and twelve, to look after each other, as they go back to look for her family. The terror of those two children, waiting all day for family that they'll never see again.

Fat tears roll down my face, and I press my hands to my eyes, stemming their flow. When I wrap my arms around Jam's neck I don't know which one of us I'm trying to console.

From the worst of realisations comes one of the best afternoons, just listening to Jam play. I request any song I can think of, holding on to this moment as long as I can.

Later that evening, after dinner, we're congregated around an organic mismatch of chairs and tables in the restaurant. Malee had brought out a range of snack dishes steadily for the last hour, and we'd been topped up with beers. Jam orders me an iced coffee, too, which the night air called for. I wasn't a big fan of alcohol in hot weather. And even heading towards nine pm, the heat was uncomfortable. I raise my glass to him, and balk as Charlie knocks a bottle of beer over my skirt. His hands are immediately on my thighs, pawing at the sticky liquid with the hem of his shirt, which only he couldn't see wasn't the best solution. Alex shrieks with laughter and Tomas finds a cloth from the bar, mopping up the liquid on my seat. I wring my skirt out, knowing that the thin fabric means it will dry quickly.

'I'm so sorry, very sorry,' Charlie whisper, a little too close to my ear.

'It's okay. At least we're not on a January day in Birmingham, eh? The heat will dry it out shortly.'

'You're a good woman, Elle.'

I nod and turn my back to his proximity, chatting with Tomas on my right hand side. Jam moves his chair around so we became a three, discussing films. I miss Lucy even more so – she can talk about films all night.

My mind wanders as Jam and Tomas discussed the merits of one particular film maker. I focus on the area Charlie walked towards, in the direction of the sea. I sip the rest of my coffee and have a sudden image of a bloated Charlie being beached tomorrow morning. I slip away to follow him, so I can direct him home.

He's meandering along the dimly lit pathway, towards the shore.

'Charlie.' I call out, increasing my strides to catch up with him. He spins around unsteadily, but remains upright.

'Elles-bells.' He responds, his arms suddenly around mine. I hadn't realised what a grip he has, my arms flat against my sides.

'Char-' I start, interrupted by his snake-lips on mine.

I work my knee free and jut him as close to his groin as I can without really hurting him.

'Elle?' Jam's question pulls Charlie away and I step aside.

Charlie chooses that moment to throw up, and I skid away in time, holding on to my balance lest I fall against a rock and knock myself out.

'Time to head back, Charlie-boy,' Jam calls out, guiding him away from me but steering clear himself.

I follow behind, my flip-flops a staccato back drop in the suddenly still night air.

22

Jam

End January

We hadn't seen much of Charlie the following week. I know, because I wanted to talk to him, like I hadn't wanted to talk to any man before.

I could sense a growing restlessness within me. I'd been on the island almost three months this time, longer than the six to eight weeks I usually spent. But I missed performing at big shows and creating music with Cain. He was developing decent production skills up in his studio and there was some new equipment I was almost ready to try out.

Almost.

I looked out across the sea, to where the girls lived. Alex had left with Tomas earlier, both carrying a day pack, off on another of their adventures. I text Elle and asked her to meet me at the harbour, told her to pack a small bag and wear a swimming costume.

Half an hour later I'm sat on a small fishing boat, watching her confused expression as she approaches, looking all around for me.

'Down here.' I call out.

Shielding her eyes with her hand, she glances to the boat and starts laughing.

Ok, she might not have been expecting this.

'Let's go snorkelling.' I yell.

'Absolutely.' She steps easily into the boat, waving hello to the captain as she settles down on a seat.

We sail for about an hour, to a good spot, away from tourist boats. Elle easily fits her flippers and mask and dives off the boat before me.

Why haven't we done this before?

I dive off and swim alongside her.

Blue and yellow and silver-tipped fish swim around us, and I can see Elle grinning through her snorkel, giving me the double thumbs up, as she glides through the multi-coloured schools. She would love snorkelling in southern California, would probably be a natural diver, too.

I keep an eye out for jellyfish, careful to be in Elle's vision when I tap her shoulder to show her something in the water. After about ten minutes, I'm the first one to raise my head into the sun, taking off my mask and enjoying deep breaths, my feet kicking below me. Elle sits up a few minutes later, imitating my moves.

'This is incredible, Jam!' She enthuses. The captain smiles and waves to us. 'I can't believe we haven't done this before!'

'I know - you're a natural.' She is the most fearless woman I know.

'Will we see sharks?' She sounds more curious than worried.

'There might be a few leopard sharks, or black tips about, but they won't bother us, unless you catch yourself on coral.

'Say no more, I've seen enough shark scenes. I'll take extra care. Are you going back?'

I nod, replacing my mask and waiting for her to replace hers. Then I hold up three fingers, counting down to one and we both sink under the water, our legs stretching out behind us.

When hunger and tiredness collide, we return to the boat for lunch.

The captain hands us towels and cleanser, takes bottles of water from the ice box. The three of us settle into a pasta lunch, followed by fresh pineapple, sat in the best kind of silence from people who enjoy simple food and good company.

We set off back to the island just before the sharks will get hungry. Neither Elle nor I want the day to end, and we sit on the sand in the fading sun, enjoying the warmth of the dying day before dinner.

I've never felt more sure of any step I was about to take.

23

Elle

End January

Jam and I sit watching the sun sink below the horizon, our bodies drying on the sand after a mesmerising day.

Gliding through the water today, watching multi-coloured marine life carry on as if we weren't there was unreal. I couldn't hear anything, could only dart my eyes this way and that, trying to take in as much of this new world as I could, with Jam right beside me.

I had felt so calm.

The whole day had been unlike anything I'd experienced; just the two of us out in the middle of a perfect blue sea.

After our afternoon snorkelling we'd climbed back on the boat exhausted. It felt like we were just drifting back to shore, without any sense of purpose or urgency. Time had frozen for us.

I never thought I'd find anything to replace the euphoria of shopping.

Jam turns to face me.

'Elle?'

'Hmm?'

'I need to be honest with you.' He states.

'Okay. I wouldn't expect anything else.' His hand reaches out, covers my knee, and I'm stilled. He lets his hand drop.

'Please. Just listen.'

I can't say anything. I wait for him to continue.

'Do you remember being in Cornwall together, when you got into trouble swimming?'

'Kynance Cove, near Lizard Point.' I'd never been in such trouble in the water before.

He nods, his arms wrapped loosely around his knees. His eyes never leave mine.

'One moment we were swimming together, the next you were laughing at me for cutting our time short. You'd promised to head back for lunch after another five more minutes.'

That April day, all those years ago, before I'd moved out to the US, was carved in my mind. The balance between safety and danger is a knife edge.

'I'd been looking for you, from the beach. And I couldn't see you. I kept looking for this pink sign.' He reaches out and tucks a strand of hair behind my ears, his hand lingering. The action seems wildly deafening, but my cheek turns towards the warmth of his hand. His fingers rest on my face.

When had our bodies become so close?

'I sensed you were in trouble, and came back out. I was almost too late, though.'

I couldn't tear my eyes from his chocolate brown depths.

'I don't know what I'd have done if you hadn't come up.'

I struggle to speak, find myself leaning towards him.

'That was just the first time you saved my life.' I whisper.

I feel the kiss coming and curiosity pushes me ever so slightly towards his mouth.

His salt-drenched lips are cool on mine and my nerve endings roar awake.

No, no, no, 'we shouldn't be doing this'.

'Why not?' he murmurs, and I realise I've spoken aloud. He pulls me closer, his lips eliciting a slow growl from somewhere new inside me. His fingers cup the back of my head.

I have never had a first kiss this good.

Never.

Never.

No.

NO.

I drag myself away, my disorientation mirrored in his eyes, and land my finger on his lips as he's about to speak the unspeakable.

But his mouth parts and he softly suckles my finger. I'm stunned, transfixed by his eyes, his action. A sound from somewhere behind us pauses his movement, allows my thoughts to finally air.

'I can't lose what we have.' I sob, pulling my hand back.

Seconds later Tomas appears. Lovely, sweet, oblivious Tomas. I stand abruptly, wave goodbye to Tomas and leave, so that Jam has no choice but to stay and talk.

I ignore dinner.

How can I face Jam, knowing that he wants something from me that I can't give?

We've spent so much time together, practically naked with the amount of swimming we've indulged in, especially today. We've crossed into something that can't happen. I don't know where my future is, but it can't be in Nashville. I can't traipse around after him, when I don't know my own fate.

I get ready for bed, pretend to be asleep when I hear a soft knock at my door. I'm grateful that Alex isn't here so she can't let him in.

When my phone pings his message through, those three words tear open my heart.

I email Nancy Adams and ask her to book me a flight to London, then pack up Thailand, silently sobbing at how I've ruined one of the best friendships I've ever had.

24

Jam

End January

I haven't been able to sleep all night.

I've really messed things up between us if she didn't reply to my message. And who the hell sends that kind of message, instead of telling the person you love to their face, so they can see the sincerity of your expression, so you can hold them and explain why you had to say what you'd just said? I love you doesn't need to be reciprocated with the same words. I had to share the truth in my heart once I knew it was there. I hadn't even hoped she may feel the same.

As the sun rises, I walk past Elle's apartment, hoping we'll bump into each other on our morning walk to the shore. Malee stands at the restaurant doorway.

'Good morning.' I nod to Malee as she stretches awake, a broom in her hand. She smiles and steps forward.

'She gone.'

I stop walking. I don't need to ask who.

'I saw her early morning, in a tuk-tuk with case. First ferry out. She gone.' She sweeps the porch steps. Don wanders out eating breakfast. He waves at me before settling, blurry-eyed into a chair, staring at a TV screen.

'What do you mean, Elle's gone?' I whisper. 'She wouldn't leave without saying goodbye.'

Would she?

Maybe she was just a girl who was only ever here on vacation?

Malee softly places her hand on my arm.

'Elle is a good person. Not ready yet for more, maybe. Give her heart time to grow to the size of yours.'

I know the words are meant in kindness. But, in the middle of the night, Elle has left Thailand without saying goodbye.

And just like that, I have to go, too.

I stride to the Andaman Sea, watch the shoreline do what it always did, and know it is no longer enough.

25

Elle

Early February

If I'd tried to say goodbye, I would have ruined whatever friendship we'd built.

He will just have to understand that some people are only in our lives a brief time. Apart from Lucy being married to Jam's boss, our paths don't have to cross again.

As the plane takes off I look out of the window, at the country below me where I've lost, and found, a piece of myself.

If I'd gone to Jam's room at midnight, like I really wanted to, I would have lost even more of myself that I knew I had to offer.

I pull my eye mask down, and put my headphones on, for escapism; it will be a long while before I sleep again.

Ten tear-stained hours later we touch down at Heathrow.

The customs queue is blissfully short. I'll soon be on a bus to Cornwall, to who knows what. I officially had nowhere to call home; my belongings fit into two bags, and I was sleep-deprived and hungry. At least I hadn't had to wait for the baggage carousel.

As the departure doors open I see Nancy waving at me.

What on earth?

'Elle, when I get a call from one of my children in the middle of the night, I know something's up'. She wraps me up in a hug I didn't know I needed, and half-carries me to her car.

I sleep all the way to the end of the country I used to call home.

When I wake, I'm under a white duvet, in one of the guest house bedrooms. A small, square, vintage alarm clock on the bedside table suggests it's just after ten; the sun greets me at the window, so it's possibly morning. I have no idea which morning.

I want to stay in bed all day and also go in search of coffee. I don't want to appear rude to Nancy, but I just can't talk. I want to curl up and stay here forever and not think about what I'm going to do with my life.

I doze on and off until just after one, possibly on the same day. There's a quiet knock on the door.

'Elle?' Nancy's soft voice.

'Hmmm?' I struggle to sit up. 'I'm decent.' I call out. Although perhaps only just; I can imagine what my hair and face look like.

Nancy carries a tray, with a huge mug of coffee and a plate with an oversized sausage butty. I move up so she can sit on the bed next to me, and I place the coffee on a beach-hut themed coaster on the bedside table.

'I know what a long flight can do to a body – Cassie always sleeps for a couple of days when she comes back from Asia. Joe and I don't need as long to recover after our cruises, but that's just because we idle the day away on holiday, whereas you two have been working hard.'

I nod, grateful for the distraction of the delicious butty. Just the right amount of tomato sauce to peppery sausage, too.

'Anyway, I thought you might like a little snack. No need to get up, though, you sort out that jet lag. I'm making a casserole for dinner this evening, there'll be some set aside for you.' I finish my mouthful.

'Nancy, thank you. For picking me up. For looking after me. I have no idea what I'm going to do.'

'About what?'

'A job. Money. Life.'

'Oh, they all sound like big questions for a Wednesday. Take as long as you need to. This room's all yours.'

Tears start, catching on my throat. Nancy carries on smiling. Then hugs me as the flood takes hold. I miss Lucy so much, I've messed up a good friendship, and here is this lovely woman, catching me as I fall.

I sit back, smiling through my sticky face, spent.

'I'm going for a walk if you'd like to join me? Feel free to use anything in the room – it's the place Cassie ends up in after her travels. She keeps a case of clothes under the bed.'

I nod and she leaves the room so I can finish eating, and then try to make myself physically presentable.

We walk to the headland and the wild Atlantic Ocean. The wind whips all around us, meaning we don't have to talk much. I've borrowed one of Cassie's woollen hats and some jeans and a fleece, my Thai wardrobe woefully inappropriate for an English winter on the coast, even if it is the south west coast.

But the walk helps to clear some thoughts. I'd done what I had for a good reason, and have no regrets that threaten to have me heading back to Heathrow for a flight; I'm no good at goodbye, and didn't trust myself around Jam. And I'm not cut out to be a Teacher of English as a Second Language. I wished I could have said goodbye to Malee and Don, but I would send them a parcel in a few weeks when I could think clearly.

What on earth I was capable of, though, I didn't know. Social media and event management hadn't exactly been my dream job after all. I wasn't sure what events were being held nearby that I could help with, either. And from the last time I came here, I knew that we were off the beaten track a little.

The last time I came to Lizard Point had been for Lucy and Cain's wedding, but that had been at the end of a summer, long days of parties and dancing and keeping the groom away from his guitar, until Lucy asked him to play the song, the first song they'd written together. A stab of memory slices through me as I remember when we'd all been in the cove together the year before and Jam had hauled my cramped body out of the water. I hadn't known then about the loss of his parents to the ocean. I'd pushed myself further out to sea, probably in some vain attempt to show off my swimming abilities.

I tune back in to Nancy's chatter about the wildlife and the weather, as we make our way back to the guest house. She doesn't seem to mind that I don't offer much in conversation, and she doesn't ask me any questions, preferring instead to talk about the imminent arrival of her fourth grandchild, my second niece or first nephew. I don't think I have enough in my bank account for a flight to Nashville. I need money as a priority.

Back at the guest house I put the kettle on for a pot of tea, and Nancy slices up a homemade carrot cake, which I have a second slice of with little hesitation.

'Now, this afternoon I'm going to finish my needlework. You're welcome to join me, as it's good to have the company. Or you can catch up on more sleep. It's up to you.'

'It would be great to watch you craft, you are so talented. I love the throws and cushions you took over to Nashville.'

'Oh, I have great fun with my imagination. Have you ever worked a needle?'

'No. I can't sew a hem on a pair of trousers. Lucy can, though, she's more practical than I am. More creative, too.'

'Well, the height difference in you two - I bet you never had to hem a pair of trousers.'

I laugh at her accurate analysis and follow her into her craft room.

'Wow.' I stop at the door and she turns to face me.

'Oh, I know, I know, my mind likes to do a variety of projects, often all at the same time. I'm trying my hand at crochet, but I find coordinating the yarn feels funny beneath my fingers.'

Floor to ceiling shelves fully occupied three walls, filled to the brim with books and art supplies and cute inspirational ornaments and hangings. Underneath the window was a vast desk, with a sewing machine set up and a radio in the corner.

Nancy pulls out a wicker basket from a shelf and settles herself into a teal, padded, swivel arm chair, which looks far more appealing than a standard black office chair.

I sit on a small sofa, tucking my legs underneath me, pulling my long sleeves over my hands, out of comfort not cold. As my eyes adjust to the contents of the room, organisation in the chaos revealed itself. Hardback books spill out of one set of the shelves, their spines revealing art theory, quilting, dressmaking, knitting, crochet, jewellery making, basket weaving and embroidery. Nancy's desk is wide and the centre of her creativity, bordered by sewing accessories like a stuffed tortoise masquerading as a hedgehog, thanks to the metal quills.

Nancy unfurls a piece of navy material out of her basket, a large lilac hoop in the centre. She shows me the picture she's creating - a brush-stroked mantra declaring a crafter's domain had its own order - in a selection of white and pale blue threads.

'I love the relaxation I feel when I'm embroidering. Well, any craft, really, but I keep returning to embroidery. I don't follow patterns, though I keep buying the books. The project feels more natural, more organic, if I'm creating as I go.'

I murmur in a positive way, not willing to punctuate the calming environment with two-way conversation. Nancy seems happy to natter away, and I continue my gaze around the room. Fabric is stored in lidded plastic crates, hand-lettered labelling announcing projects on the front that read more like family members. Shelly and Jason: king-sized quilt; New Grandchild: cot bedding; Cassie: travel luggage.

My eyes begin to drift closed, and my body sinks further into the arm of the sofa. Nancy stands, reaches for a pastel pink and lilac quilt, and lays it over me. The reassuring weight of the cover nudges me into an afternoon nap.

I wake, startled, from swimming alone, terrified.

A familiar smell hits me.

'Hello, lovely, I've just made us a pot of tea.' Nancy pulls a hidden table towards my side of the sofa and I struggle awake. Evening has fallen, and table lamps have been switched on in the room. The radio plays quietly.

'I'm so sorry.'

'No need to apologise for sleeping – it's your body's natural way of fixing itself.'

By the end of the weekend, after more sleep and more food than I've probably enjoyed all year, I begin the Monday morning search for work.

I don't know anyone in the UK anymore, and I'm not quite ready, or able, to turn up on Lucy's doorstep, not with the imminent arrival of the newest family member. The nearest towns to the Lizard rely on tourism, and Easter is still a few weeks away. Nancy has said I could borrow one of their cars, so I could travel further. Falmouth and Penzance are the nearest towns and Truro the nearest city – all around forty-five minutes to an hour away. I concentrate my searches in these places, sending off CVs and covering letters to anyone, in the hope that they're looking for office staff.

By the end of the first week I've had no bites.

'Why are there no jobs available in this whole county?' I exclaim one afternoon, in my room, as I receive yet another email from a hotel saying they aren't hiring. Has the whole of Cornwall decided to boycott the digital age, binning social media and search engine optimisation?

I push back my chair from the desk and the laptop, and pace the guest room that Nancy has offered me for however long I need. The views are stunning, and I feel the most relaxed I ever have. However, tourist season is on the way, and I can't take up a paid space at the guest house, nor afford to live off part-time seasonal work, I've realised. I've been so good at standing on my own feet for so long that I can surely do it again. I turned up to Boston with nothing, and look what I created.

I collapse onto the double bed, clutching a cushion to my knees. I'd had everything for years, the best education, the best network, a job I loved. Even managed to live in two countries in two months, which was probably some kind of record and certainly one that employers should see in a positive light. Or, maybe they think I'm a flight risk? How had I gone from everything to nothing? Just one wrong movement was all it had taken, for the house of cards to come crashing down on me.

Two, if I counted the gallery disaster.

I unplug the laptop and sit on the bed, resting against the pillows and handmade cushions, and search for Fion's gallery. What else was the egotistical toe rag up to? The website I'd created still hasn't been updated, still advertising Sunny's launch. He should have at least taken that down. Fion was so too-faced; we had both known that any publicity was good publicity.

I check LinkedIn and update my profile, to Actively Seeking, adding Tim and Jake to my professional network. Looks like they've CrowdFunded the research project they were keen to do and I'm really pleased for them. It feels like a lifetime ago that I'd sourced a hundred thousand dollars in funding for the gallery's project. Why was looking for a fifteen thousand pound a year job in Cornwall so difficult?

I updated my profile to living in Cornwall. Tim sent a message thanking me, again, for understanding about their reluctance to come to the launch. Would it had have mattered had they been there?

Good question.

Was Fion a ticking timepiece just waiting to go off at someone?

Boston was amazing, but I couldn't have afforded to live on the Cape for just light housework, like I was doing here. And the Lizard has just has many stunning views as New England's seaside towns.

I reassured Tim that I was well, just resting after travelling.

Then a message from AJ: You're moving around a lot lately.

Yes.

Avoiding or recharging?

Enjoying.

Come see me when you're next in Boston.

No plans to leave England for a while.

Anything I can do to persuade you?

Teleport this location to Boston?

I send photos of Lizard Point and Kynance Cove across, and then upload to my feed.

Okay, maybe I'll come to you.

Aren't you working?

I write anywhere.

I'm not in a place of my own yet.

Okay, let me know when you are.

I send him a thumbs-up and close down my laptop, going in search of Nancy to see if she needs help with anything. Before I had everything dry cleaned, I used to be able to iron okay; I'm sure I could still do that now.

I find Nancy in the kitchen, dancing along to a familiar album – Cain's first one, I think.

'Oh, hello. Do you fancy learning how to make Cornish pasties?' she asks.

'Sure, especially if we can eat one afterwards.'

'That's why we're making them.'

The music is upbeat, the counter chaotic and there is the most divine smell already coming from the oven.

'Nancy, I must take a photo of this for your blog. The light is great at the moment.'

'For the what, dear? Take as many photos as you want while I put the kettle on.'

'The guest house surely has a blog? Here, let me take a photo of you.'

'Okay, but I'm not doing my hair.' Nancy looks her usual deliriously happy self, and this time flour covers her face, from when I'd dropped a bag near her.

'You have a website, yes? So guests can find you?'

'Oh, yes.' She pulls out cups and a huge tea pot and I snap more photos. 'Jason set one up for me a few years ago. He kept on talking with words I couldn't quite put my finger on. My mind may have wandered.'

'I'll have a look after lunch and we'll see where we're up to. These photos would look great.'

After we'd tidied, Joe joins us for lunch, declaring the pasties the best he's ever eaten.

'That's very sweet of you to say, Joe. Really, it was the teacher, not the student. I'm much better at ordering food in than cooking it.' I reply, laughing. I enjoy their relaxed conversation, could see how these loving people had raised my brother–in–law.

After the second pot of tea is empty, I help to tidy up, and then excuse myself to the bedroom to look up the website details. The page has a style from 2010 all over it, which said that a business had to have a website, but it didn't need to be looked at ever again.

I jot down some thoughts and go through the house to speak to Nancy. She's in her craft room.

'I've had a look at your website and there are a couple of things that would look very good on there.'

'Oh, what's that then?'

'Well, this is a family business, and everything is locally-sourced or handmade.'

'Absolutely, this is what our guests come to expect.'

'Well, more images would look great on the website, like today's photos, for example.'

'Okay, if you think that's a good idea. Why don't you get in touch with Jason, and he can tell you about any technical stuff you might need – I'll go with whatever you suggest.'

'Really?'

'Of course. You know much more about this than I have a desire to learn.'

I grin and bring the laptop to the craft room. It doesn't feel right to be cooped up in the guest room.

Jason replies to my email quickly, saying the domain is paid for, but he's lost the will trying to ask his parents to update it. We talked through some ideas, as this would one day be his business, and he was enthusiastic about the family-approach. I had a green light to go with my experience, and he was there if I needed anything.

I thought about how I'd helped bring in writers for the Nashville Narrator's writing retreat. The personal touch was definitely the way to go, although, at Cain's insistence his name wasn't mentioned. He hadn't wanted the project to be undermined by anyone who wasn't necessarily interested in writing, but only his name.

We needed some more information for the website. I spent the afternoon researching local events, and advertising them on the guest house blog and social media pages. We didn't need to create any events, just to share the nearby ones.

As I expected, Nancy had a good digital camera on hand, so I went out for a walk to snap a fading sun and the dramatic sky over the Atlantic. I've never really paid much attention to landscape, but west Cornwall is stunning.

Back at the guest house, I upload the photos to the laptop's hard drive. I don't need to edit the photos too much. I share the images online and make a note of the follower numbers; I would grow their audience before tourist season began.

By the end of the first full week of blog posts and hours spent on Twitter, Facebook and Insta, I draw up an easy-to-read spreadsheet and line graph, to show Nancy and Joe how their social media profiles are growing and what likely impact that could have on their business. They generally had half-occupancy throughout the year, starting in March, but only full occupancy part way during the summer, as they spent more time with family, and their grandchildren came to visit. Financially, that was what they planned for and they were indeed a family business. But I could perhaps help build their occupancy for the other months, from tourists who would enjoy the bracing walks and homemade food, perhaps even a craft workshop. I was starting to feel a little better about not paying my way.

After a delicious steak dinner that night, with Nancy's gorgeous apple pie for dessert, I went to bed feeling full and happy for the first time since I'd arrived in Cornwall.

I still had no idea what the future held, but I slept well that night, with no dreams of Jam and his deep chocolate eyes.

26

Jam

February

The island was smaller now that Elle had gone. And I wasn't pleasant to be around in the final two weeks of the semester.

I tried hard to keep my thoughts to myself when I was teaching and the music helped, the enjoyment on the children's faces as they worked through songs, used the instruments to tell their stories.

The other expats tried to distract me in the evenings, too, but I'd had too much of a routine that had never appealed to me; work, drink, play, repeat.

Every time I look at the ocean I miss Elle. A hole had opened in my heart; it was beating, but barely.

Sunrise and sunset with Elle had been something I'd needed, and I'd followed the path to her easily.

Staying indoors hadn't helped much; I needed to be outside.

It was time to leave.

And do what?

Move to Nashville; inland.

I'd given my notice to the school, and I was leaving tomorrow. One last night out, to say goodbye, and then I was bound for the States.

I stumble across the sand, the day's beers taking their effect on numbing my senses, on my way to my apartment, but I didn't fall.

'Wait up, Jam. Need some help finding your bed?'

Alex was under my arm, her hand reaching around to find my waist.

I was too drunk to speak, but not that drunk I couldn't observe her attentions.

We walked the short distance to my front door, my thoughts struggling with information I knew I had to concentrate on.

Alex chatted on excitedly, interrupting my thoughts. At my apartment she somehow extracted my key from my back pocket and opened the door. Her hands felt the wrong kind of too-familiar, sending shockwaves through my skin. I lean on the door frame, reluctant to go in and unable to move away.

I look down at my feet; I don't know where else to look.

'Jaaaaaaammm.' Alex sings out, grappling with my arms to pull me in.

Where are the other expats when I need them? Where's Tomas?

I'll be helpless if I cross this threshold. I look out towards the ocean, hoping for inspiration, the sound of the surf calling out.

I wouldn't swim well tonight; I wouldn't spot any signs of danger until it was too late.

'I need to say goodbye to Tomas.' I offer, heading in the direction of his apartment. 'He left early.'

'Jam.' Alex's tone was sharp. Urgent. Oh, shit, I recognised that sound.

Just keep walking, I urge my feet. Left, then right, then repeat. Do nothing else.

Was she going to follow me?

I wasn't going to wait around to find out.

I mean, she's lively, but she isn't Elle. I know how it feels to be lured in, and I wouldn't want Alex to feel like I did in an hour, when I walked away.

I couldn't hear any sounds behind me. But I couldn't see any lights on in Tomas' apartment. Maybe I'd find Charlie. Or Malee. I circle around the darkened apartment, and well away from Alex's place.

I walk until sunrise and say goodbye to Thailand for another year. If I ever returned.

27

Elle

End February

The guest house blog was doing well. Traffic had been steadily growing, and I'd found plenty of content to share. Now it was time to convince Nancy to plan some craft workshops to deliver.

Work was a great distraction from sleepless nights and I was used to fourteen hours in front of a computer, where I was in control, exhausting my mind into oblivion.

'What's your favourite craft, Nancy?' I asked her as she was sewing one day.

'Oh, I like all of them, but I just dabble. No one would pay to watch me yak away while I'm twirling a needle.'

'You have some great skills that a lot of people don't have. I really think once you see people responding to your workshops – gushing over something tangible that you've help them to create for their home, well, you'd love doing the workshops, too.'

She considered my thoughts for a minute, dunking a shortbread biscuit that I'd watched her make earlier, into our second cup of tea this afternoon. I imagined cooking and baking workshops would also go down well with guests.

'Well, what craft would you like to learn?'

'Pardon?'

'If I'm going to help people craft then I'm going to need to know what people are interested in.'

'Ah, I see where you're going. I don't know? Why don't we start with embroidery?'

I'd watched Nancy often enough this month – how hard could it be?

Oh my god, needlework was so difficult. Who knew there were so many names for sewing? And they all looked the same when I'd finished with them. Nancy's pieces looked gorgeous. She had infinite patience, but I was a rubbish student. I could see what I wanted to do, but I had no idea how to translate it to the fabric.

'Let's try something else, Nance.' I suggested. It didn't take her long to put away our hoops.

Apparently, I was dire at any craft that involved yarn, too. Knitting was far too complicated. Crocheting sort of evaded us both, even though only one needle was used, called a hook, Nancy kept reminding me. I tried something called needle felting, but honestly I just kept stabbing my fingers, and the needles had little nodules on, which meant I was being really inventive with swear words.

I didn't fancy taking on a dressmaking project, and I imagined that would take up too much space for a workshop, too.

'Why don't you two go out for a walk, maybe inspiration will fall on you?' Joe suggested one afternoon, as Nancy and I sat in contemplation. I really believed these workshops would be beneficial to the business. Maybe Nancy needed a student who was already capable of something artistic, so they just needed to adapt their skill set?

The days were becoming a little longer, and the clocks would go forward an hour in just a month, with tourists not far behind.

We walked away from the headland, alongside hedges, waving to cyclists and to car horn beeps from the neighbours. As usual, my thoughts started to settle when I found myself in nature. I think being in Thailand, away from the cities I was so used to, had helped me to connect visually with the world around me.

Gulls swooped around us, and we took a path off to the left, following the coast line to a familiar destination.

Kynance Cove.

Nancy wasn't to know. And I didn't want to run back. This was land and it wasn't going to disappear because it reminded me of losing a friend.

I somehow kept walking and breathing.

It helped to only stand on the top of the headland, though, and not actually hike down to the beach.

'This place is breathtaking.' I said.

'It gladdens the heart, indeed.' Nancy responded.

I took out my phone to capture some photos of the Atlantic Ocean and lush green fields. 'I wish I could capture this somehow in art.'

Then at the same time Nancy and I faced each other.

'Painting?' I asked hesitantly. Her smile told me I was on the right path.

'I know a couple of watercolour and sketch artists. I'm sure they'd be happy to meet you and perhaps even host a workshop. And I could just provide the space and tea.'

'Absolutely marvellous idea.' I exclaimed, high fiving her. We stared out over the water as the light changed, watching the clouds scatter, and the pinks and oranges explode. I'd loved every single sunset I'd seen with Jam, and was grateful for them all.

When we got back Joe was dancing around the kitchen, holding the phone.

'Lucy's had a baby girl. At home. All doing well. Apparently Cain is gadding about the place like a very happy papa.'

My hand flew to my mouth. I had another lovely little niece.

'Em, they're calling her Emily.' He added.

I had never wanted to see my sister so much. Time to get the artists on board and organise some workshops. Then I was going to find some digital work online, if I had to spend the next month completing opinion polls for air miles.

The first artist I met with, Mo, was the sketch artist. She'd moved from London ten years ago, when her daughters had gone to university, and spent a month at the guest house, using it as a base to discover her favourite parts of Cornwall. As soon as she visited St Ives, the bay with the best light in western England, she knew where she was going to live. She'd kept in touch with Nancy ever since and was a keen member of the thriving Cornish art community.

As agreed by Mo and Nancy, I was to be the guinea pig student. If it meant workshops would happen, I would even take on needle felting again, but hoped I wouldn't have to.

We set up our easels in the garden, while Nancy poured tea and watched us. Mo was a natural teacher and this time I wasn't as bad a student. She gave me a selection of pencils, explaining their different uses, and told me I just needed to focus on one thing and draw around that. By the afternoon I knew I'd found my favourite craft.

Nancy and Mo nodded as they examined my sketch of the lighthouse overlooking Lizard Point, commented on how I'd shaded in the sun over the outline of the lizard cliff face, creating my own memory of the area. Now I really need money coming in, because as soon as I returned from Nashville, I'd shop for my own art supplies.

Ever the decisive team, we had scheduled the first workshop for the following Saturday. Thanks to copious amounts of baking from Nancy, shopping for art supplies from Mo and online promotion from me – and a distinct lack of sleep all round – fifteen people turned up for the first art workshop and expressed interest in returning.

Over a celebratory Cornish gin or three that evening, Nancy, Mo and I planned the next three weeks of events.

Then they told me we'd split the commission equally three ways, which meant I could finally visit my sister.

28

Jam

Early March

I'd been back from Thailand for only a fortnight, but the jet lag had wiped me out.

I normally took a day or so to rest, went for a run, cleared my head, then went right on back to the studio or to the stage.

But I was exhausted. Maybe I'd caught a bug on the flight over? Maybe I was in the seasonal 'flu stage.

Yeah, maybe that's what this feeling was.

Cain and Lucy's second daughter arrived a few days ago, and I stayed away, not wanting to pass on any germ, I told myself.

I couldn't settle to anything. I found myself sitting and staring, not really seeing what was in front of me. I could be inside my apartment, looking at a wall and not realising that I'm still looking at that wall until I'm numb from sitting. Then I have this sudden rush of energy and I have to go out and run it off.

Or I could be on the porch outside my house, staring into the forest, watching the light fade behind the trees and I only go in when it's almost too dark for me to see my way back to the door.

Even now, I'm staring out of the window, not quite sure if it was time to make a meal or go to work. My sleep was off, too. Probably didn't need it after staring into nothing for who knew how long.

In the studio today, Cain had commented on my absence. My timings were good, but he had a feeling something was up. Seb had nodded in agreement. I just told them I was probably coming down with something, and we called it a day. That could have been after lunch, or before dinner, I didn't know.

I rose, stretched, and went upstairs to change from jeans into running gear. Then I just hit the ground like Forrest Gump and ran. I ran towards the park and through the gates, into the wooded haven, my feet pounding into a rhythm that I hoped would drive out the emptiness in my head.

I found myself at the falls and stopped to listen to the sound of the water crashing down.

Elle's memory surfaced and I struggled to regain control over my breathing. It was like someone had cranked the temperature up and I held on to the railings, my knuckles turning white.

'What is it with you?' I hollered.

Two passing hikers just kept on walking, ignoring my outburst.

'There's been absolutely nothing from you! I didn't want to feel the way I did, but I do. Did. Who the hell knows?'

The sun cleared the clouds, and a realisation filtered in. I was pissed that Elle had just abandoned me, too.

Lighter, I ran back home, changed, and slept well for the first time in weeks. I may still not have heard from Elle, but I could explain my dark mood at last.

29

Elle

Mid-March

I was so excited to see my brand new niece and my scrumptious toddling niece. Even Nashville might be okay to hang out in again. But I knew at some point in this fortnight I'd bump into Jam.

I'd hoped that our visits wouldn't coincide, however, I knew Cain was finishing off a record, and Jam lived nearby. But, I couldn't wait to see my family any longer.

I'd focus on seeing Lucy, on seeing Emily and Charlotte.

And not the fact that I walked away in Thailand.

Even if it had been for self-preservation.

As the Uber wound its way to their home, I'd forgotten how empty the outskirts of the city felt; from the neon, noisy, fiddle-playing centre, we were in the tranquil hills in only fifteen minutes.

The car pulled up on the wide, gravel drive and Lucy flew out of the door to greet me.

'Oh, my god, Elle, you look amazing!'

'Hi Sis, so do you.' We gripped each other in a hug. I'd missed her more than I realised. So much had happened since last summer. 'Where are my gorgeous nieces?'

Cain came out to retrieve my luggage, followed by the curly-haired cannon ball Lottie. She smelled so good, like fresh summer peaches. Cain wrapped his arms around me, asked about my flight. But as Lucy and I walked arm in arm through the house, I knew Jam was here already. In the living area he sat on the sofa with the tiniest baby, swaddled in pink.

I nodded in greeting, and he reciprocated briefly. My temperature dropped from his icy stare.

I didn't trust myself near him.

I excused myself to the bathroom, gathering my thoughts and emotions. What had I expected, after walking away, without an explanation? How could I voice feelings I was still unsure about? The last month of sleepless nights had probably caught up with me, too. I splashed water on my face and wondered what the next two weeks would bring.

When I returned to the living room, Lucy sat rocking Emily and Jam was nowhere to be seen. Cain brought coffee through, and a slice of Lucy's key lime pie, and I settled down for cuddles with my beautiful two week old girl.

For most of the following week Jam and I successfully avoided each other.

Cain was working in his studio, with Jam and Seb most days, taking advantage of me being with Lucy and the girls, so he could finish the album. It wasn't released until late September, but he wanted everything cleared before their US festival appearances and their UK tour in the summer. I'd never seen Sarah work so hard on booking gigs and arranging radio and online interviews.

One afternoon, a strikingly gorgeous blonde woman wandered through from the studio, a guitar case over her shoulder. A brunette followed just behind her. I suddenly knew what Lucy meant by there being a lot of woman in the place.

'Hey Bonnie, Patty.' Lucy smiled easily, carrying baby Em to them.

'Oh, we just wanted to say bye.' The blonde whispered.

'And Bonnie here wanted another hello with this cutie pie. You and Cain make the most beautiful children.' The brunette, Patty, said. I spotted Lucy's blush as she turned slightly towards the kitchen.

'Of course, you must have cuddles, ladies, would you like some tea?'

'You two sit yourselves down, and we'll make it.' Bonnie declared. She smiled at me, then, and I think I momentarily questioned my sexuality. But her warmth overshadowed any physical attraction. She clearly had excellent DNA and was a sweet woman, too, as both women stood their guitar cases down and headed into the kitchen. Lucy and I went through to the lounge to sit, where Lottie played.

Bonnie and Patty spent the afternoon happily playing tea parties with Lottie, cuddling Em and just catching up with us. Patty, at Lottie's insistence, played guitar and sang some nursery rhymes. Lucy was transfixed, as was I – I would happily hear nursery rhymes on the radio if they were sung this way. I'd have to get her album details from Lucy – I was sure Nancy would love her sound, too. She sang contemporary country classics with such a clear voice.

When Cain and Jam joined us, I smiled but volunteered to take Em up for her bath. I figured a squirmy newborn would be easier to handle than trying to avoid Jam's glares. Lucy followed shortly, and I retired to my room with a headache. Trying to eat with Jam nearby would have certainly brought one on.

Then, one night, Cain asked if I'd mind looking after Em and Lottie with Jam, while he took Lucy out for dinner.

I'd be left alone with Jam.

Of course I couldn't refuse. Or feign death.

I helped Lucy get ready in their room.

'Sis, you are a bag of nerves.'

She stopped pacing her dressing room.

'I can't help it. I've been fat for so long – oh, I know, I know, it was pregnancy, it's different. But nothing feels right. Does that make sense?'

I stand, gently separating her wringing hands, lest she end up like Lady Macbeth.

'You are gorgeous, you are a fabulous Mummy of two, and you're going on a date with the guy half of Nashville is after.'

She dropped down onto the sofa then, her legs splaying like a new fawn.

'Don't I know?' She cried. 'Oh, I trust him with my heart and my family. But it doesn't stop people trying.'

As the story unfolded of just what kind of year Lucy had gone through, I shoved guilt at not being here for her aside, to be dealt with later.

I brushed hair away from her eyes.

'Have you told Cain how you're feeling?'

She shook her head. 'The words have never sounded right in my head. I couldn't explain my feelings to myself any more than him.'

'Tell him you're jealous of how many women love him as much as you do.'

She cackled then. We both knew that would get through.

'Elle. When did you become so smart?'

'Oh, I'm a long way from that. Come on, let's find you something in red.'

Half an hour later, after I carefully applied make up to watery eyes and smoothed out her hair, Lucy was looking good, even if she was still feeling wobbly on the inside.

The way Cain looked at her, though, as they walked through the house, her arm linked through his, my heart constricted at their connection.

In the lounge, a freshly-bathed Lottie, wearing Elsa pyjamas, was turning the pages of a picture book that Jam was reading to her. Em was sleeping in her basket. I sat on the sofa and listened to the tale of Pooh Bear and his friends. I picked up a drawing pad and a blue crayon and started drawing lines. I looked down to realise I was looking at Kynance Cove, the distinctive curve easy to read off the page.

When the story was finished Lottie climbed into my arms, rested her head on my shoulder, and we climbed the stairs to her bedroom. I tucked her in, read another story, gave lots of cuddles, and watched as she fell asleep.

In the lounge, Jam had made coffee for us, which I smiled and took gratefully. I sat on an armchair, tucking my legs under me, and peered down to a still-sleeping Em.

'Are we going to talk?'

'I don't know what to tell you.'

'What happened?'

What happened? I realised how much I wanted you and how it would ruin everything; yeah, because it was now so perfect, wasn't it?

'I had to leave.'

'Without a goodbye?'

I was grateful for the burning sensation of coffee. He sounded so hurt. Even after all these weeks.

'I had to leave.' I repeated. 'We can't happen.'

He nodded, but didn't look convinced, or that the matter was over. It would have to be.

'Lucy looked good.' I tried a distraction.

He nodded again. I couldn't look at his face. Just saw him rise and head towards me.

I looked up, startled.

'Yeah, well, it was a shitty thing to do.' He downed his coffee and walked out of the room.

Yeah, yeah it was, I agreed to his retreating back.

When Em stirred an hour later, I gave her cuddles and her bottle. I changed and washed her, found a clean sleep suit, and resettled her in her nursery. Jam was nowhere to be seen and I wasn't in the mood to look for him. I couldn't.

The doorbell rang, as I was on my way downstairs. I frowned at the late hour, but this was Nashville, and I figured a would-be attacker wouldn't be so polite.

A young girl, red hair resting on her shoulders, and the roundest face I'd ever seen stood there. A jeep was parked, no other passengers in. She held a basket in her hands.

'Hello?'

'Is Cain in?'

'And you are?'

'A friend. He helped me. I'd like to give him this. And, and for Lucy as well.'

I stared at the woman. My instincts did not like the situation. Would it have been different if it had been daylight?

She held the basket out further. Some chocolates and a sealed pot of something and an old book. No clocks or ticking sounds.

'I'm sorry it's late, I'm a bit of a night owl. I could come back tomorrow?'

Half the music industry worked during dark o'clock.

'I'll take it. Will he know who to send the thank you card to?'

I couldn't take my eyes from her face.

'It's okay, we're friends. The book will make sense.'

She handed the basket over and as soon as I took it she darted back into her jeep.

I stepped back inside, closed the door and put the basket in the hallway.

Minutes later Lucy and Cain returned home.

Before I could ask how their evening was, I saw her tear-streaked face. And Cain's pinched face. I smiled, gave them an update on their girls, then gave a fake yawn and said I was going to bed.

Before I'd closed the door, Lucy came flying in to my arms.

What on earth? Was I going to have to floor my brother-in-law? I would.

Through sobs, Lucy told me their evening hadn't been great. They'd eaten, but conversation had been too polite. Had she run out of interesting things to say? Who was she anymore? Cain had reassured her, had complimented her, but she'd been so disconnected. And he'd had more messages that he wouldn't explain.

'Sweetheart, you've just had a baby.' I sooth, 'There are all sorts of hormones and emotions running through you right now. You just need time. And a massive bubble bath, and a cup of proper tea.'

She wiped her tears, nodded and disappears to her room to undress. I run her bath, pouring generous amounts of bubbles in, but when I return to the room, she is curled up on the bed fast asleep. I cover her up, turn off the light and slip out of the room.

I find Cain at the piano and join him.

'Is Lucy okay?'

'She will be. Just keep loving her.'

He nods furiously. 'Every single day.'

'Good. Otherwise we'd have to have a chat outside.'

He roars laughing then and we hug.

My fingers sail across the black keys, making up their own tune. Cain's fingers echo their story.

'I wish I'd learned piano.'

'You still could.'

'Nope. Not at all musical.'

'Jam could teach you.'

My fingers stop their wistful movements.

'There isn't an instrument he can't play.'

I'd never heard a truer statement.

'He's busy.'

'You two okay? Haven't seen you in the same room this week?'

'Hmmm.' I whisper.

'I'm here if you want to talk.'

I rest my head on his shoulders while he plays a ballad I know he'd written for Lucy.

When I look up, I see Jam walking away.

I wish I could take back his hurt. I sit up and rub my eyes.

'Oh, one of your friends was round earlier. I mean, literally, her face is enormous. No offence. She left a basket for you, which I put in the hallway.'

'Did she say anything?'

I shake my head. 'No, I hoped it was something you knew about.'

'Okay, thanks.'

He remains at the piano and I make my way to my room.

The next morning I wake unsettled from a dream I'm not entirely ready to wake from. I can almost taste salt water on my lips, though I don't know whether from the Andaman Sea or the Atlantic Ocean.

I dress with heavy limbs and head to the kitchen. Lucy and Cain are dancing to an eighties film soundtrack – something about cutting loose. They're so caught up in each other, I feel like an intruder. And I am; I have no place to call home any more.

I feel Jam stand behind me, literally caught between that rock and a difficult place. Can't go forward, can't turn around and collide with a man who looks at me like he doesn't like me very much. Any other friend and the old me would have cut them with a glare and ignored them. But you can't choose your family, can you?

'Anymore coffee in the pot?' Jam slides past me into the kitchen, his shoulders cutting through me. He chats so easily with Cain and Lucy. The feeling that I'm an outsider is new on me, and I don't like the density.

'Come in, come in, breakfast is almost ready.'

'Luce, you make the best breakfast.' I plaster on a fake smile to make it through the meal and sit at the table, thankful when Jam sits at the furthest end. Lottie is in her big girl chair, happily gnawing on apple slices. Just another couple of days before I can return to England; perhaps inspiration of my future would turn up on the flight home.

After breakfast I shoo Lucy and Cain away with their girls and tidy up the kitchen. I'm more than a little startled when Jam offers to help me. I continue with that fake smile, the one that doesn't quite reach my eyes, and start to clear the plates from the table.

30

Jam

Mid-March

It had been five weeks since I'd last seen Elle, and everything about her had changed. She was no longer the strong-willed woman who took on challenges as instinctively as breathing.

It only made me need her more.

Each time I moved close to her, like a gazelle she loped away, helping Lucy with this task, twirling Lottie in the air, cuddling baby Emily. I couldn't get near her.

Frustrated, I spent much of my time in the music room.

It was on one such session that Cain turned up, as I was midway through The Foo Fighter's Pretender. I knew Elle wasn't playing games, but it felt good to play the rock song. I finished the track with heavier breathing than normal.

Cain handed me a beer, which I downed half of immediately.

'So.'

'So.' I repeated.

'You've found the elusive Mrs Jam.'

'What?'

'I don't know who she is, but I've never seen you this edgy. Ever.'

My secret was still safe.

I nodded.

'It'll work out.'

How the hell was that going to happen, when I couldn't get five minutes alone with Elle?

'Meet her in Thailand? That why you came back with so much energy to run every day?'

'Yeah, something like that.'

I really wanted to be angry with Elle, for the way she just left me in Thailand, without saying goodbye. But I didn't have to be a genius to work out how vulnerable she looked. The confident young woman who back flipped across a bar for a bet wouldn't have recognised herself in the tired, awkward young woman that skittered around trying to avoid me.

I told her how I'd felt, expecting to be challenged, but the closed response I got threw me into confusion. The more I watched her, stood close to her, I knew I had to apologise for being, as Cain would term it, an arse.

At breakfast this morning I'd had to brush past her. I'd felt her tension, her inability to move and I had to break this circle we were doing around each other. Cain and Lucy were playing with their girls, leaving me and Elle alone in the kitchen together. She passed me the plates to stack in the dishwasher. An ordinary domestic act, but she was as nervous as a beginner on a surfboard off the coast of Portugal.

'Elle.'

'Hmm?' She turns her back on me and I see her shoulders hunch. I want so badly to sooth the knots out of her muscles.

'I was startled when you left Thailand so suddenly.'

Her shoulders tighten further and she busies herself with wiping invisible crumbs from an already clean work top.

'But I think I understand.'

'Oh?' She doesn't look up, her hands move up and down the worktop, as focussed as I am when I'm waxing my board.

She shifts to another part of the kitchen and I wonder if she'll run away again.

'I never had the chance to finish my thoughts on the island.'

'Jam, please.' Neither of us moves. Hearing her beg my name on her lips, I couldn't have moved if the room had been on fire. Unless Elle was in danger.

I pressed on. I had to try to fix us.

'I love ... our friendship. I love ... spending time with you. I love ... your obsession with Pad Thai. I love ... your energy for adventure.' I daren't say any more. Will she take the lifeline? Would I believe myself with these half-truths? I love everything about her.

'Jam.' She falters, her eyes finally on me. 'I love ... how you're going to forgive me for being grumpy towards you.'

She steps forward, wrapping her arms around my waist. Her cheek is warm against my chest. I fight with resting my chin on her head, holding her in my arms and never letting go. 'I can't stand tiptoeing around you.' She whispers. 'You're one of my oldest friends.'

'I'm only a few years older.'

I love the way she laughs. The way her shoulders settle down a little. At a possible renewal of our friendship?

'I love … how you'll forgive me for not being able to say goodbye. I've always just walked away.'

She releases me and my arms fight with reaching out for her again, as she steps back, smiling briefly, then turns and continues to tidy the kitchen.

It was enough.

For now.

31

Elle

End March

It was my final night in Nashville, before heading back to the UK. Lucy had ordered stacks of pizza and made her famed key lime pie.   It was easier being around Jam, since we'd talked, but our ease in Thailand had gone; wrapping my arms around his waist had somehow felt final.

   I was looking forward to having time to myself again, without the anguish of personal thoughts to deal with. I doubted that we'd ever go back to our easy nature around each other. Too much had been said that couldn't be unsaid. I still hadn't worked out how he'd gone from feeling nothing for me, rejecting me when I offered myself to him at the end of the summer, to feeling everything and telling me that he loved me. For the first time I did not feel comfortable with the attention and I'd run away from him in Thailand, because I couldn't say goodbye.

   I wasn't sure what he meant to me; he was my oldest and closest friend.

   He was the man I'd followed to another country.

   I'd only ever led, never followed.

   Had he meant everything to me, when I had nothing to offer, and was a stranger on a new continent, his friendship a much needed balm when I was hurting?

No, he'd been there when I had everything, too. He was dependable, that's what he was. The family member I could rely on when I'd been in trouble.

And then I'd gotten us both into trouble by kissing him.

Cain rested back in his chair, his forearm leaning on the wooden back rest. He was clearly content with dinner as well as life. I watched the easy chat between him and Jam, a pang of jealousy from missed times, being an insider, that I no longer was.

The talk turned to what my plans were in the UK. I'd only really thought about going back to Nancy's guest house to help out, there was nothing else planned.

'What about your house in Newquay, Cain? Didn't you say you needed someone to look after it?' I pretend not to see the arm squeeze Lucy offers him, by way of an *I'll-explain-later* scenario. He nods and Lucy continues.

'It's been so long since we visited it, we need someone to list any repairs. Maybe look after the garden.'

I laugh, nearly choking on the sip of juice I'd just taken.

'I am many things, Luce, but I am not a gardener.'

'No, but you could organise for the garden to be sorted. I remember we needed new decking - and didn't we talk about redesigning the vegetable patch?' Lucy squeezes Cain's arm softly again and he nods.

'Would you like me to get some quotes?' I smile.

'You could stay and oversee the work, if you like?'

My sister has a way about her.

The next afternoon, Jam volunteers to drive me to the airport. I hesitate, but I accept the offer.

I sling my backpack easily into the trunk, and climb onto the passenger seat, with the week's worth of travel food Lucy has organised for me. I keep my limbs firmly away from his.

We drive in silence most of the way, and I'm lost in thoughts of what I'll do in Cornwall when he starts talking.

'I know you'll be looking after Cain's house when you get back, but I wonder if you could look in on mine?'

'Oh, yeah, you have a house in Newquay, too?'

He nods. 'Before Lucy and Cain moved out to Nashville, Seb and I agreed to relocate to the UK. Seb was happy living in London, but you know me – I need to be near the ocean. I love the beaches in Cornwall, and the music scene of Newquay, so I bought a derelict house not far from Fistral beach, and worked on it. I rent it out during the season, but it would be helpful if you could look in and let me know any work I need to organise.'

This man was prepared to uproot his life for his loyalty. For my sister. He's never going to be out of my life, is he? And who wouldn't want a dependable friend?

'Of course I will, Jam, it's what friends are for.'

'Yeah. Friends.' He agrees, as the night closes in on us, his eyes on the early evening road ahead.

I manage to sleep for a few hours on the night flight to the UK and pay attention to a film. I make my connecting flight to Newquay, without having to hurry and Nancy is waiting for me at the airport.

I catch her up on her gorgeous granddaughters, how well Lucy's doing, how hard Cain's working to finish the album. She's already planning their summer visit, with trips to the nearby animal parks and picnics exploring the coves. I think she may have forgotten he'll have shows to attend. I wished I'd grown up with Nancy. I never allowed myself to think about what-ifs; they really don't help. But she is so warm and caring that it's hard not to wonder. But I'm glad I'm in her life, however I wandered in.

As soon as the car pulls up, Joe envelopes me, and over pots of tea, scones, jam and clotted cream, I show them the photos and videos I took of their family. They video call Lucy and Cain, and I head to Cassie's room to unpack. I catch up on emails and the guest house blog, check bookings are okay for the first watercolour workshop, which will be held in a couple of weeks, over the Easter weekend.

The emotional turmoil of the last couple of weeks finally takes its toll and I crash out early evening, transforming an afternoon nap into sixteen hours of sleep.

I spend the next two days with Nancy and Joe, sorting out jet lag and making sure Mo has everything she needs for her latest workshops. Then I tell Nancy I'm heading to Newquay to look over Cain's house, and if it's okay, I'll stay there, sorting out repairs. I know she'd let me stay forever, but I don't want to take up room. And I already know there would be no chance of me paying the going rate.

'That's a marvellous idea!' She exclaims, 'Newquay is a lovely spot for youngsters, and only an hour away. Take my car.' I've never seen beyond the airport before, but she assures me it'll agree with me. And I agreed to return once a week, for Sunday lunch.

When I pull up at Cain's house, I'm thankful I've brought a sketchpad with me. The detached building overlooks the longest stretch of golden beach and rolling tide that I've ever seen. According to the signs this is Fistral Beach, and a quick Google informs me this is one of the sites of Boardmasters, the annual surf and music competition held each August. The town is small, but absolutely perfectly formed and visually stunning, with white-washed or pretty pastel properties overlooking the ocean, luscious purple and pink flowers draping over garden walls. I'm going to enjoy adding these colours to my sketches.

Inside the house are four generously-sized bedrooms, two of which are en-suite. The style is musician, with guitar references everywhere. Still, this is the town that celebrates music, so he obviously found renters of the same mindset. The open-plan kitchen and living areas are spacious, made cosy with a sofa I could get lost on and furniture that could easily be pushed aside for entertaining.

The front garden is compact, could possibly do with some trimming, but then the real outside space is the ocean. The back garden has great structure, with a decking area that looks like it captures plenty of sun. I'm an expert, but even I could see that there isn't much work that needs doing beyond mowing, or tidying the shrubs. A pink blossom tree sits in the centre of the lawn, and I imagine lying underneath it on a blanket, dozing off to the sound of busy bees. The Elle this time last year, cramming for last minute exams, between evening gallery showings and sorority parties and networking dates, would have balked at such a waste of a day. I'd never set my senses loose as much as I had these past few months.

I collect my bag from the car and move my few things into the smallest of the rooms, change the bedding and clean through the bathroom. For lunch I sit at the breakfast bar, enjoying one of Nancy's steak pasties, and a whole pot of tea, daydreaming the afternoon away. After I clear up I head to Jam's to look over his place, just a few minute's drive away, according to the GPS.

I thought I loved being in Cain's spacious house overlooking the Cornish surf, but as soon as I pull up on the wide drive of Jam's detached Victorian, at the top of a hill, the sun setting on the headland, I know in an instant why he bought the property; an upper living area suggests a one hundred and eighty degree viewing platform.

I hurry up to the well-maintained front garden and unlock the cobalt blue door. I'm greeted with a spacious hallway with a curved wooden stairway, which

I take almost two steps at a time, as I make my way to the upper level.

I'll explore the rest of the rooms later, but right now I just want to look at the view. In the substantial open-plan bedroom a huge bed sits on the right hand side, a corner sofa and a small wood fire on the left. Two sets of French doors lead to a decked garden area, which makes me feel as if the ocean just belongs to me.

I find the key to the first door and step outside as the fireball sun begins to sink below a dusky blue Atlantic. The swell of gentle surf plays with a few horizontal black-suited surfers and paddle boarders. I inhale the salty scent, and catch an additional fragrance to my right. Turning around, I find thriving lavender plants spilling along the wall.

I take out my phone and snap a few images, from one side of the headland to the other, which I'll send to Jam later. As darkness descends, solar powered floor lights start up. I can only imagine what this house would look like on a warm spring evening, filled with people and laughter.

When it's too dark to see the water any more I step back into the room, closing and securing the glass doors. I sit on the sofa and find low level bookshelves, mostly containing hardback biographies of obscure musicians. I riffle through a few pages, content just to enjoy the peaceful surroundings. I spot a door partially hidden by a pillar. I wander over and pull open the door revealing an en-suite worthy of any spa. A double shower and a roll top bath vie for attention. The thought of who could have joined Jam in the hidden room makes me feel as if I'm intruding, prying on memories, and I softly close the door.

Stomach suddenly growling, I reluctantly leave the converted room and look through the house. I find three further double bedrooms and two bathrooms on a lower floor.

On the ground floor the lounge is a haven for post-surfing chats around a wood fire.

The dining room overlooks a previously manicured garden, which will look glorious again with a swift and thorough tidy.

I lock the house up, promising myself I'll return tomorrow, with art materials, and I drive back to Cain's, calling in to a restaurant on the way, for a fish and chip supper.

Tomorrow I'll call into a hobby store to select my first acrylics, following detailed instructions from Mo. I have to paint the view from Jam's roof. It will look perfect in the writing retreat. I haven't seen that much visual inspiration in one place since I'd left Thailand.

32

Jam

April

I used my cell phone as just that, to make calls. I still preferred to use my laptop to check and respond to emails and to respond to messages on social media. I'd learned that having a phone in my hand too much caused deterioration in creativity. When I had to open my laptop I was making a conscious effort to log in, communicate, log off.

One afternoon I noticed I had a few emails from Elle, and opened up the first one, which I recognised as a photograph of the right hand view from my house in Newquay. I was treated to six more images, making their way across to the left hand side of the view, which looked out over the expanse of beach, the setting sun glistening over the ocean. Elle had typed a message of practicalities and assured me that absolutely nothing needed doing to the property.

Reading her messages made me almost long for the English home I'd fallen in love with, which now accommodated the first woman it had ever seen. I could only imagine Elle's face if I suddenly turned up in her reverie. We might never go back to the way we were, but I certainly wasn't going to ruin anything by turning up unannounced.

I caught up with a few more emails about gigs and interview requests then logged off, and went in search of Cain in the house. We only a few more months until the album launch and I knew there was no way I should leave Nashville until then.

Patty and Bonnie came over to hang out, write and chat at the retreat quite a lot now. They migrate towards the house with their guitars and notebooks to work, with Lucy often found nearby.
    Cain and I joined the three women, and the two girls, just before dinner most nights. Lucy sat contentedly on the couch, baby Em in her arms, or in her basket, and we all took it in turns to play with Lottie, or make dinner.
    Sarah and Seb were on their way over tonight and Lucy had invited Tallie over, so dinner was being taken outside. I stood at the grill wrestling steaks; Cain was in the kitchen, taking care of the potatoes and salad.
    Bonnie came over to see if I needed a hand. The Bluetooth was playing Fleetwood Mac and I'd just taken a sip of my beer, so I shook my head no, smiling. She turned her attention to the cocktail bar, setting up a pitcher and pouring in measures and ice. I watched, fascinated. As she worked she sang along to Stevie Nicks on *You Can Go Your Own Way*. She had a fantastic voice. I jammed out as I turned the steaks, and she set down a raspberry cocktail next to me.
    'Oh, nice.' I exclaimed after almost downing half of the raspberry gin drink. 'Clearly, cooking is thirsty work.'

'Do you cook a lot?'

I shook my head. 'I eat more than I cook.'

'I drink more than I cook.' She grinned, raising her glass to me, before she sauntered off to the table to set the pitcher down.

Sarah and Seb arrived and he took over the grilling while Sarah helped Bonnie create another cocktail pitcher and what looked like a mint mocktail for Lucy and Lottie.

Cain brought out enough food to feed a small army – but then he knew how I ate, followed by Patty, holding Lottie's little hand, and Lucy with Em in her arms. Tallie carried out dessert.

I plated up the steaks according to almost-alive for Seb, absolutely annihilated for Patty and somewhere in between for the rest of us.

Em had lots of cuddles from everyone and she didn't seem to mind them at all. Lottie sang nursery rhymes with Patty and twirled Bonnie's hair between her tiny fingers, bringing out her Barbie dolls for comparison. The evening was easy; Lucy and Cain had created an amazing family. I couldn't quite see myself as a father. I roamed far too much.

'Is there always this much food when people visit?' Bonnie grinned, pushing her plate away so she could no longer pile it high.

'Always. Arrive starving every time.'

'Thanks for the tip. Y'know, I always had Cain down as an arrogant singer, but he really knows what he's doing, doesn't he?' She acknowledged.

'Yeah, Cain knows what he wants and he goes for it.'

'And what about you. Do you know what you want?'

I turned to study her face, but I didn't sense an agenda there, just a willing listener.

'I think so. But knowing and having can be oceans apart.'

'Yeah, I hear that.' She raised her glass and we chatted about her upbringing just outside Chicago, how she had always wanted to write, how she was glad Sarah persuaded her to come up to the house with Patty that day.

She was so relaxing to talk with.

But she wasn't Elle.

Seb came over to us and the conversation turned to Bonnie's work. She'd only been in Nashville a few years, was still building her songs. Wasn't sure if she wanted behind the scenes or on-stage, travelling everywhere.

'How did you and Sarah meet?'

'We met in another lifetime.' Seb drank some of his beer.

'What, now?' Bonnie leaned in for the story.

'We actually met in a bar in East Nashville. I was playing for an up and coming artist – I hadn't met Cain at that point. Sarah had. She was in the bar with friends that night, and when we took a break she came up to me, asked if I'd like the good news or the bad. I asked for the bad, and she said we'd known each other hundreds of years ago and had missed out on so much time together.'

'And the good?' Bonnie asked.

'Well, we'd just met and we had the rest of our current lives together.'

'And it's been ten years since we've been married.' Seb reached over to kiss Sarah, and I saw that familiar look on Bonnie's face. We were both ready for the same connections.

Except, I'd lost mine.

33

Elle

April

I woke in the guest room at Cain's, to a stream of sunlight warming the bed. Pulling back the curtains introduced me to a cloudless sky, the promise of a beautiful spring day ahead. The first thought I had was returning to Jam's home to paint. I dressed quickly, piling my new equipment into the car. I stopped at a bakery for fresh croissants, picked up a large mocha and drove straight to my new happy place.

With the easel and acrylic paints set up on Jam's rooftop garden, I pull my sunglasses down over my head and settle into a flakey, buttery, croissant, sipping my coffee while I look ahead and look around. I was so new to painting; I knew what I wanted to capture, but I didn't know how. Mo told me that she pushes thought to one side and just lets her creativity take over. The more I thought about how I would approach the project, of painting the panoramic view of Fistral Beach, the more the light would change. A cloud drifting across could interrupt this image I wanted to recreate.

I finished the pastry and nipped to the, frankly gorgeous, en suite, wash my hands and return to the canvas. I pick up a medium sized brush and just go for it; I can always return tomorrow, and every day afterwards, until the piece is finished. I was learning that painting offered me that chance to evolve.

I YouTubed techniques as I went along, learning how to add white or mix colours, to create the different shades of blue I wanted to. I found that I preferred working in pastels and in blocks of colour – I liked the control, as though I was the one painting, and not the painting being painted.

By mid-afternoon, after an hour's battle with hunger, I put the brushes down and sit back. I pick up the tepid mocha, wincing at the temperature, but I'm appreciative of the lip quench. The picture isn't perfect, but I have thoroughly enjoyed the experience. I step back inside the top floor, wash my hands and, after I look in the mirror, wash the pastel blue from my face. I clean up the sink, admiring the huge bathroom one more time, wondering if one night I might be able to soak in the roll top bath. It would only be a few weeks yet before the first batch of tourists arrived. I wonder if I could claim to be an eccentric painter who needs constant access to the lavender-scented roof garden.

I went back to the garden, cleared away my paints and the easel, removed the sheet I'd put down to take care of any spillages; the decking was still pristine. I put a new, clean sheet inside the hallway and lay the canvas on the floor to dry.

Then I let myself out, locked up and drove back to Cain's house.

After a shower I pop a pizza in the oven and pour myself a small glass of Chenin Blanc, then take advantage of the unexpectedly warm evening and sit in his back garden. There are no views of the ocean from my seat, but I know it is there, I only have to look out of the windows in the guest room to see it. The blossom tree is already heavy with scent.

After dinner I find a paperback mystery on the bookshelf and wander down to the beach to watch the sun set. I sit on a wall and forget to look at the book, so mesmerising is the ever-changing view. I know once the sun sinks the temperature will drop, I can't quite leave.

I snap a few pictures and send them to Cain. I send one to Jam; it doesn't feel quite right to be at the beach, watching the sun set, without him.

Over the next few days I settled into the routine of working in Jam's garden, although I realised the daily pastry and coffee wasn't helping my waistline or budget.

I caught some great weather and spent every afternoon in Jam's garden, exploring different art techniques I'd admired in other artists, mixing the colours until I had just the right shades. I was comfortable with the straight, clean lines, working with the image of the sea, rather than detail. I'd enjoyed studying the bold colours and clean lines of the Pop Art paintings from British painter David Hockney, in undergraduate art electives in my first year. I was beginning to identify with his appreciation of a west coast. That year was when I'd started to think about working in a gallery.

Nancy rings one night, and after catch up about our daily lives, she asks if I'd like to show a few paintings at a gallery in Newquay?

'I don't think so, no, I'm not that good.'

'Well, Mo was talking with her local art group, and one of them, Rock, holds a spotlight session in his gallery each month on new talent. She showed him our website and the work you'd shared, and he really liked it. She was so excited on the phone just now'.

I continued preparing my pasta dinner, vaguely remembering an evening when I'd uploaded a couple of pieces I'd played with, of the Lizard coastline - more to keep the content updated for the website, so Google didn't pitch a fit with rankings.

I hadn't expected that an artist would like the work.

'I bet you already have several paintings that you could show. Wouldn't it be a fun adventure? And you never know where it may lead?'

And I'd be helping out Nancy and her friend.

And I had been looking for local art exhibitions to share on the guest house site. I just hadn't expected to be the referral.

The microwave dinged and I pulled open the door, letting the steam settle.

'Oh, go on, Nancy. Tell Mo I said yes. And to send me the details'.

I rang off and curled up on the sofa with my bowl of cheesy penne, a small smile starting to spread on my face at the realisation of the work ahead; I knew what it took to prepare for a showing and I wasn't throwing anything less into my own. I wouldn't be sleeping for a while, so I probably needed a double-chocolate brownie tonight, with clotted cream vanilla ice-cream.

Then, I had to paint four new pieces for the deadline in ten days.

I painted at Cain's, at Jam's and headed back to the Lizard for new perspectives, practising techniques on paper, until I found a style I was happy with. When I wasn't painting, I poured over more online videos to develop the skills so I could create the scenes. I hadn't been as exhausted in so long and slept briefly, and heavily, each night because of hard work.

I visited the gallery a few times, and had found a lovely little studio in the back where I could organise my work and sketch out future projects. I'd shadowed the gallery assistant, Beth, for a couple of afternoons, getting a feel for the gallery. It was smaller than Fion's gallery, but infinitely more welcoming.

When Rock realised I'd previously worked in a gallery in Boston, he asked me to cover a couple of mornings, after the showing, whilst Beth studied. He would pay me for my time, too, and I had free reign to position works, or commission artists if I found something I liked.

Lucy was ridiculously happy for me, and wanted video footage of the event. I promised her an original painting instead, needing no technical problems, after what had happened in October. Only six months had passed, but so much had changed. I'd changed; I was spending so much time by myself, which brought me more joy than city-dwelling networking ever had. That had been all I had known.

On the day before the showing, I photographed the exhibition and sent the images to Lucy. Then, ever the social media manager, I uploaded to my own socials, happy-dancing around Cain's house as the likes increased dramatically.

Maybe I had my own creative talent.

I replied to a couple of messages from Zed, showed him what I'd created, and he promised he'd commission a piece for his new office; he was already a senior buyer, and I was so pleased for him.

Tim and Jake congratulated me on my first show, asked if I was returning to Boston. I said probably not this year. They'd branched out into commercial property development, as a way of building for their future. I was just looking forward to surviving tomorrow. I set the alarm on my phone and switched it to airplane mode, then settled down for a disruptive night's sleep, thanks to adrenalin.

When the morning finally arrived I was filled with nervous nausea. Certainly more nervous than if I had organised another artist's work. I drank half a cup of strong tea, repeating to myself that nervous energy was a positive sign.

The weather was a typical British seaside day – a storm was forecast in the afternoon, and the town was grey from head to foot. I was glad my canvasses were already at the gallery. I dressed in three quarter length trousers and a long-sleeved tunic, and my long waterproof coat, then drove to the gallery, humming seventies rock to myself to quell the giddiness that threatened. This was no time for fight or flight.

I found a parking space just outside, grateful that I didn't have to walk, and entered one of my new favourite places. Beth smiled as I walked in and burst a party popper over her desk in celebration. The pop startled me, but not as much as her bear-hug.

'Happy show day'. She sang.

'Thank you, Beth! I love your enthusiasm. I could only imagine how Fion would have reacted had I set intentional noises off.'

'He sounds no fun whatsoever. Tea or Coffee this morning?'

I hang up my coat and ask for coffee, taking a seat at the till. I tried not to stare too much at the front door.

Beth continued reading her notes for a class and I took lots of photos for the gallery's website, promoting the business on social media. It had always felt constructive to work online, I had lived with my phone switched on day and night for so long. But it also felt strange not to be wielding a paint brush.

I repositioned my smaller pieces, talked with any customers who came in. But they were just in for a browse and probably to stay dry for a while. Beth had her lunch in the back office and when she returned I retreated to the back room and busied myself with the guest house social media. The climb in followers was growing quickly and I knew this would lead to increased bookings.

Each time the bell tinkled, I was on tenterhooks, expecting a call from Beth to speak to a potential buyer. But as the rain eased off, so did the doorbell.

I was lost in my work when I realised a tall figure stood in the door way. It took me a moment to realise who it was.

'Jam?'

34
Jam

Easter

It didn't me long to find the gallery, at the top of a narrow street in the town. I opened the glass-fronted door, to a soft tinkle of a bell, ducking my head to clear the framework. The assistant at the till looks up and smiles as I step inside, watching as I straighten my back and shoulders. Then she returns to her phone screen.

Elle is no where around.

The open space is warm and welcoming, the thick sandy carpet reflecting the nearby beach in texture and colour. Turquoise walls and subtle overhead lights reflect on canvas paintings. I move closer to one, a large landscape of a white lighthouse, overlooking a windy headland, another one of a large Victorian hotel overlooking a beach. I like the simple lines and block colours that the artist has chosen.

As I walk around the space, I realise there's a corridor at the back, with an open door way at the end. Black and white photographs, of railway stations and trains, on a white wall flooded with natural overhead light, literally move me along to the room.

My breath hitches.

Elle sits on a small sofa, sketch pad in hand, her dark brown hair tucked behind her ears. I almost don't want to disturb the concentration on her face. I step into the space, and she looks up startled, then a hesitant smile on her face.

'Jam?'

I nod, looking around as I walk towards her, then stop.

'Is this your new office?'

'Yes, but what on earth are you doing here?'

'I missed Newquay. And Lucy has been non-stop excited about your showing. I had to come and take a look for myself. Good view.' I point towards the double patio doors, a neat urban garden and an ocean backdrop. 'I'd like to say you couldn't draw this, but you probably could'. I turn back, catch Elle watching me.

'I was just about to organise coffee, would you like one?'

'I don't want to interrupt your work.'

'You've come all the way from Nashville to find the ocean. I'm sure I can shout you coffee.'

I smile and nod, following her into the shop, which was somehow positioned at the back. I didn't understand British architecture sometimes.

'Beth.' Elle took money from a small wallet. 'Can you head down to Lorna's for coffee? And possibly cake?'

Beth was out of her seat like a shot.

'I'll have a caramel latte, you have what you want, and ... Jam... ?'

'Americano, thank you.'

Beth plugs her earphones in and wraps herself in a wool coat. Elle settles onto her stool. I take a nearby one and pull it up to the counter.

'So, are these pieces all for sale?'

'Yes, and the artist is giving a generous discount today.'

'Oh, is the artist around?'

She holds out her hand for me to shake and realisation dawns as I look around the room. My fingers connecting with her warm skin brings me back to her eyes.

'You?'

She nods, as I look at the paintings differently. 'ALL of these?' I thought she may have had just a couple of pieces on an easel or something.

'There's a new artist showcase on the second weekend of the month, and this month it's me. I'm an artist.' Her happiness is infectious.

I stand and look closely at the landscapes, all using the same clear lines, same subtle pastels, with the ocean as a feature point. This time I read the little cardboard plaque, advertising the artist details, in brush-pen handwriting, and a price with three digits.

The bell rings again and I turn, expecting coffee, but it is an older woman with either a friend or a sister; they look very similar in a twilight-glamorous appearance.

They chat away to each other, calling Elle over, and I carry on looking at the images around the room. They are all mostly of the Lizard peninsular or the Newquay coastline. I'd love a painting for my living room, reflecting the view from the opposite window.

The door bells rings again and Beth is preceded by a younger couple in matching jackets, boots and scarves.

I retrieve the coffee from Beth, taking it into the back room, while she helps Elle with the customers. Inside the paper bag are three giant chocolate muffins, and my stomach growls in anticipation. I busy myself with the coffee and staring out of the window, at the newly growing lavender waving in the wind.

I hear Elle before I see her, as she squeals along the corridor.

'Everything okay?' I stand at the burst of energy and she stops just in front of me, waving her phone, the distance between us like a portal to another world.

Maybe I should stop watching late night sci-fi.

'I'm an artist, Jam. A PAID artist!'

'That's fantastic, Elle, congratulations!'

Instinct takes over and I pull her into the hug I'd been craving. She was back in my arms, her head resting on my chest. Thunder roars in my head and my heart. It is just a hug.

Between friends.

I step back, grab the paper bag behind me.

'Muffin?'

She grins, diving into the bag, and devouring the chocolate.

'The first couple that came in have just bought the white lighthouse, as they go to the Lizard every year on holiday. I've given them the guest house details! And Beth has just told me that my four large canvasses of Fistral have been bought online!

I turn and offer her the lukewarm coffee, 'God, I feel amazing. Someone actually bought something I created. I never dreamed I'd sell my work. It wasn't you, was it?'

She looks crestfallen.

'I promise you, Elle, it wasn't me. Although I'd like to talk to you about a commission. Let's go out and celebrate. When you've finished.'

'I'm done. It's almost three o'clock. The gallery is closing in a few minutes anyway, and no one else is braving this weather. Let's go.' She brushes chocolate crumbs from her lips and I lead the way out of the suddenly too-small space.

What I love most about British seaside towns is their abundance of public houses. Even better when the weather is atrocious and you find a good pub and stay there all afternoon.

We've had a couple of drinks and Elle goes to the bathroom while I amble over to the bar to order the next round. I lean on the wooden counter, waiting my turn, and gaze out of the wide windows to the grey outside. Grey ground, grey sea, grey rain, grey sky.

Then, a memory so invasive, my eyes sting. A similar day in childhood, about this time of year, at Uncle Eddie's house in San Diego.

The only time we visited during Easter was for Mom and Dad's anniversary. I quickly calculate; they would have been married thirty years tomorrow.

I turn back to the landlady of the pub, ask her for the same drinks again. When our ciders are poured, I try to hold my hands steady as I walk the short distance to our table.

'Thanks, Jam.' Elle lifts her local, cloudy liquid, asks what we're toasting.

'Mom and Dad's thirtieth wedding anniversary. Tomorrow.' I drink half of my cider, the sharp taste of mischievous apples going down too easily. British cider contains the kind of alcohol that can make standing up feeling like lying down. Just what I need.

Her glass remains poised mid-air, and I really don't want pity in the next sentence she utters. Her head drops to one side.

'So, you had to haul my arse out to the seaside to celebrate? To Mr and Mrs Logan.'

Attagirl.

'Bloody hell, yeah, what is it with Easter and grey seas?'

'Fending off the tourists as long as we can.' She sips her drink and I know mine is disappearing too quickly. A bubble of uncontrollable laughter threatens, and I shift my chair back, needing space to breathe. I earn a loud tut from the man at the table behind me and my head swivels.

'To day-drinking'. Elle declares, lifting her glass to mine.

I turn my attention back to Elle, and the best parents, and one hell of a good idea.

'To day-drinking.' I confirm.

Her phone vibrates and she squeals after reading a message, looking up at me with her hand over her mouth, her eyes sparkling.

'Everything okay?'

She nods, clearly unable to speak, and hands me the phone.

I read the message quickly.

'Oh, wow, brilliant news – another sale!' That deserves a toast.

'Definitely'. She lifts her glass.

'Aren't Tim and Jake from Boston?'

'Yep, they're lovely tech nerds. It's so sweet of them to buy three more paintings.'

'You know this means it's a sold out show, right?'

'Oh, shit, you're right!'

I need to always see Elle this happy.

She turns to look towards the window; the light catching her throat makes me catch my breath. She turns around and raises her glass again.

'To the great British weather.' She says, wearing her perfect smile.

'Indeed.'

35
Elle

Easter

It's been so long since I just talked rubbish in a pub all afternoon, while the cider just keeps disappearing. The rain has eased, but it's still grey and windy outside. Every time the door opens, bringing in a gale, all heads turn to make sure the door is properly closed.

'To the Great British weather!' I toast, again raising my glass.

'Indeed.' Jam clinks my glass.

He can't half drink. I watch him drown the golden Cornish cider, Rattler, steadily, purposefully. I wonder if he's forgotten that's not American cider.

Suddenly, he stands up, remembering his coat almost as an after-thought.

I finish what I can of my drink and follow him outside, simultaneously trying to zip up, hide under my hood, and catch up with his long strides.

The rain has stopped, so I lower my hood, to keep a better eye on him. He wanders down a slope and around a corner. He's heading to the sea. Not for a paddle in this weather, surely?

Dense, granite clouds loom over the sea, in the near distance the faint vertical gathering of rain. We're about to be soaked.

Keeping up with Jam with my cider-legs is an effort.

What the hell is he doing?

He stops on the sand, his head lifting to the sky, the wild tide close. I match his steps, am close enough to watch his closed eyes struggling, long lashes shadowing an already shadowed face. He's had to endure so much, from such a young age. It'll never be easier for him. I wish I could evaporate his pain.

Rain lands right on us and the rumble of thunder threatens. I swear if I see lightening we're out of here. The waves are as loud as the wind, clambering for attention like toddler twins.

Jam's arms lie limp at his side, his shoulders slumped. The weather is battering him. In two paces my arms wrap around him.

He turns so that we're chest to chest. He doesn't push me away like he probably wants to; I wouldn't go even if he did. He needs to be held. Our fabrics cling to our bodies and to each other. I press my fingers along his scalp, massaging in and out, a weak attempt to combat his blindingly obvious physical pain.

The thunder rolls ahead but we don't move from our spot on the soaked sand. I reach for his icy hands and clasp mine around his, wind clawing my fingers. I keep my head low, my mouth away from his lips.

When the rain turns horizontal, soaking my waterproof coat, I tug us gently away and he follows. I lead him along the path to his house, which in this weather is only a hasty few minutes away. At the door I fumble with the key and numb fingers. Jam rests his body on my back, the weight of him so new and yet familiar.

Once inside I strip our coats off, hang them in the utility room and push him upstairs and into the beautiful en-suite. It's like he's been drained of all energy.

'Strip.' I order, as I run a hot bath. He's confused for a moment, but as I'm closing the door his fingers reach down to unbuttons his jeans.

I dash out into the covered area of the rooftop garden, shucking off my trousers and tunic, so that I don't soak his floor any further. Back inside, I search through his wardrobe and find clean clothes for us. I'm about to dart into his other bathroom and a hot shower, to stop my teeth chattering, when he opens the en-suite door, wrapped in a towel.

'Get in, Elle, you're freezing.'

My black underwear could be a bikini that he's seen a hundred times on the beach, but I'm acutely aware it's not.

'I promise you, I haven't farted in the bath.'

Humour cracks the awkward ice and I nod, nudging past him, smiling through my shivers. I finally sink into the beautiful roll top bath, submerging my head for a few minutes, to warm up faster.

It doesn't take long for my body to heat and when I reluctantly climb out, a worn navy blue bathrobe has been left on the heated towel rail. I snuggle into the warm collar, wondering how I missed seeing this on my way into the bathroom.

I pull the door open, steam escaping behind me.

Jam has lit a fire and there are two mugs of tea on the table. He's not around, so I grab the wet clothes and put the laundry on, then head back into the bathroom to change into the smallest joggers and a long sleeved t-shirt I could find.

This time Jam is sat on the sofa when I leave the bathroom. He's wearing similar clothing, although it fits better, obviously. He's sipping tea and I settle down near him, but not too-near him, and reach for my mug.

'Thanks, Elle.'

'For what?'

He looks at me, so much on his mind, in his eyes.

'For being there.' He settles on.

'I'll drink to that.' I laugh, raising my mug to his.

'And to pizza five minutes away.' We clink mugs.

And to velvet chocolate I think, as I sip my tea, tearing my eyes from his.

We watch the fire until the pizza arrives, eat straight from the box, and laugh over a black and white slapstick comedy from the 1930s starring Clark Gable and Claudette Colbert.

'I love being here.' Slips out from my lips. 'Your garden is a fantastic place to work from.' I hastily add.

'Ahh, they were Fistral scenes at your gallery.'

'It'll be hard to stay away in the summer when your guests arrive.'

He drains his tea and I stretch my arms up, easing out the crick in my neck. Then I stand up. 'I'm going to head off; I'm feeling dry enough to walk back to Cain's. I'll pick the car up in the morning.' I tell him.

'Stay. Please. I have plenty of space. Rooms. You can stay in a room.'

I wait for the onslaught of internal refusal to kick in. But all I feel is shattered.

I nod and at his gentle smile I'm glad I did. I head downstairs towards one of the bedrooms, and climb easily into a bed. Sleep takes me almost immediately.

36
Jam

Easter

I wake, startled, acutely aware that Elle has spent the night with me.

In a different part of the house.

I didn't know which thought was most confusing.

I quickly shower and dress in jeans and a t-shirt, then head for the kitchen. Coffee. Bacon. Eggs. That's all I should think about.

I've just plated up when she appears in the kitchen, in her long top and cropped trousers from yesterday.

'Morning, did you sleep well?'

She nods, carrying our plates to the table and sipping her milky coffee.

'Brilliantly, thank you. Think the excitement of selling out my first art sale caught up with me.'

I join her at the table, forking the scrambled eggs quickly into my mouth, resisting the urge to say anything profound or profoundly ridiculous.

'Very different to selling someone else's art work?' I eventually ask.

'Absolutely. I never knew I was actually good at the creative side of it.'

'You have plans to open your own gallery, don't you?'

She groans and shakes her head. 'My ambitions were so wild, without any real substance. Just wanting isn't enough sometimes.'

'Everything happens for a reason. Maybe being on the other side of the easel is what you need right now.'

'I've had one show. And friends bought my artwork.'

'So fast that strangers haven't had the chance to see how talented you are. '

She doesn't come back with anything, just shakes her head and eats.

'Elle. Never give up on dreams. You'll have the independence you need one day.'

'Hmmm, independence.' She repeats.

How can I tell her I mean career independence only?

We finish eating, and I refill our coffee mugs. Elle asks if we can drink on the roof garden. I follow her upstairs and outside.

The weather is cool this morning, but promises to offer warmth later. The clouds will shift. Elle cradles her cup in both hands, staring out towards the ocean. I check the surf app on my phone.

'Do you fancy seeing more of Cornwall? There are some incredible beaches around for surfing.'

'You mean better than Fistral?'

'Sure, Fistral - and the Cribbar reef - are the best in the UK for surf, but that's no reason not to explore. We could take the boards. I'm not flying out until tomorrow morning.'

I can see her struggling with a response, and I'm about to ease her out of it with tales of music production work, or catching up with people, when she nods.

Slightly, but definitely.

I turn to the beach and exhale a slow breath.

Just over an hour later we pull up at Sennen Beach, not far from the UK's most westerly point, Land's End. The pure white sand and turquoise waters still conversation as I park the van. I can see the attraction in Elle's eyes. This is the closest beach in appearance to Thailand's islands.

I unlock the boards from the roof, handing one to Elle. Cain has handled that board hundreds of times, and I know it's reliable.

Elle and I settle into our wet suits, changing on the outside of the van, our focus on the horizon in front of us. Elle wears her flip flips to the beach, and I pad down barefoot. A few surfers are already out, making the most of the early, quiet season, before summer.

'Is this your first time surfing?' I ask.

She shakes her head, 'I've been on a board a couple of times'.

We wade out together into the ocean and lie down on the boards, paddling for the waves.

'Is your leash attached to your leg?' I double-check. She nods, and her positioning on the board makes me confident she knows what she's doing.

Almost at the same time, we see a wave approach. She turns easily on her board to catch it. I turn in the opposite direction, creating more space between us, and charge forward.

A barrel is forming and as the wave rises I hop onto the board and steer myself through the water curtain. Short, but satisfying. I crash into the ocean with a smile. When I come up I hear Elle laughing on the wind.

For an hour we play out in the surf and I go from full to ravenous. I look around for Elle. She's found a wave and I watch as she crouches onto the board, turning it nicely parallel, riding, a pure look of happiness on a woman owning the ocean.

When she crashes, she does so comfortably, almost immediately jumping back on the board. I paddle over to her, waving, and she paddles towards me.

'That was incredible.' She gushes. 'I'm almost tempted not to eat. But, y'know, lunch!'

'My stomach was hoping you'd say something like that.' I agree and we turn to the shore.

Back at the van I help Elle unzip. She returns the favour for me, and I scoot around to my side of the van to change. When I'm ready I sit inside, trying to concentrate on the view in front of me. A few minutes later, Elle is up in the front again beside me. She pops on the sunnies she'd worn on the way down and asks me to take her to lunch.

How had it ever been awkward between us?

I take her to my favourite beach cafe, which serves incredible pasties and we finish off with a shared scone with strawberry jam, topped with clotted cream.

'Ready for another beach?' I ask. She nods quickly, and we set off, driving north along the coast, to

Gwithian beach, halfway between Sennen and Newquay.

When I've parked we change into our wetsuits again, and I hear a lot of wriggling from Elle's side of the van, and just a small amount of cursing.

'Need any help?' I offer.

'Nope, all good, thank you.' More cursing, then the sound of a zip stalling. 'Well, might need help with the zip. Sound like a proper damsel in distress, don't I?' She says, as I walk towards her.

'Except those damsels don't handle a board half as well as you do.'

We take off along the sand, her flip-flops long forgotten, and spend the afternoon enjoying the expanse of the water. The waves aren't as big, though, and Elle is off the board more than she is on.

'Shall we head back?' I ask, and she readily agrees. Without hesitation I unzip her suit and help her out of her arms. When I've changed, I find a navy hooded top I keep in the back for late afternoon post-surfing and hand it to her. She pulls it on gratefully and I turn up the heater on the short drive back to Newquay. The CD starts playing and Muse fill the rest of the journey.

As we near, she asks if I can drop her at the gallery to collect the car, then she'll head to Cain's. That is probably a very good idea.

As I pull up on the drive, Elle thanks me for a lovely afternoon and hops out of the van. I tell her she should keep the hoody until next time. I watch her climb in and close the door, then drive away as the sun begins to settle over Newquay.

37

Elle

Easter

After breakfast with Jam I fully expect to go back to Cain's to change, and carry on with some more painting. But then he suggests surfing and I don't hesitate. I've been on a couple of trips to LA with some classmates and hadn't been able to resist trying out a board. But the beaches had been crowded, and I was the only one who wanted to go out. I had felt so lost yet happy in the middle of the ocean and I wasn't going to pass up the opportunity to surf with an expert.

I have to know how many more beautiful beaches Cornwall is keeping secret from me.

I'd only been to Kynance Cove and Fistral, both stunning in a different way.

But Sennen Beach could have been around the corner from our Thai island, with the same hue of blues and white sand.

Except, I know this water will be considerably colder.

I change easily into my wetsuit, glad that I'm wearing a long top as I remove my cropped trousers and climb into the suit. I ease the middle of the suit up, and coordinate slipping into the top half and discarding my clothes. I'm once again grateful for gymnastics classes. Although, look at the trouble that brought me.

The board that Jam offers me is light, obviously looked after and rounded, which will give me good control on the waves.

The Atlantic Ocean is a very understated chilly, but I just keep moving, wading in until I lie on the board and paddle to the waves. I bet Maui would be fantastic; even Lucy had gone paddle boarding out there with Cain. And I'd love to see more of the Californian shoreline.

I'm ready for my first wave. Aware that Jam is watching me intently, and like a student in front of teacher, I don't want to show either of us up. Although, technically, it had been a Brad out in Venice Beach, LA, who had taught me not to embarrass myself on a board.

I hop easily up onto this board and manoeuvre myself so that I'm parallel, tilting back as the wave approaches. And for a few seconds I'm in the same happy place that I find when I'm painting. As the wave breaks I dive into the water and prepare for my next.

A couple of times I just coast on the board through the wave, watching Jam steer his body effortlessly along the waves, like the board is a natural extension of him. I bet he would be fantastic to watch in a surf competition.

My body aches, that special kind of happy ache, and I paddle towards Jam with lunch on my mind.

Clambering out of a wet wet suit isn't much fun, especially with the cool air on your body. Jam unzips me, and I pull his zip down as far as I dare.

I know stalling is a bad idea, so I shift myself out of the wet and into the dry as quickly as I can. I'm already dreaming about the pot of tea with lunch, and maybe asking Cain if I can take one of his boards out on Fistral.

We arrive at a cute beach cafe, which serves the biggest pasties I've seen. But, after a morning of diving in and out of the sea and jumping on and off the board, I have an appetite. We opt for sharing a huge scone. I don't think I'll ever stop enjoying sinking my teeth into the weight of cool clotted cream.

I wondered if we'd call it a day, but when Jam suggests another beach, I'm curious.

Gwithian beach feels isolated. The stretch of sand and sea is almost endless. I expect that even in tourist season there would be room for everyone here.

I manage to get back into the wetsuit, with just a few choice words. But I hear similar vocabulary from Jam. Those waves look good, if further out. I take off running across the sand with my board, forgetting my flip-flops in my urgency to keep warm. Jam is right with me.

I spend more time in the sea than on the board, though. I sink my arms into the water and paddle quite a bit, and when the sun is above my back it is lovely. I could close my eyes and imagine drifting around forever. Then the clouds cover the sun and my teeth set off chattering. It's time to call an end to a perfect day, even though I'm not supposed to have perfect days with Jam.

He is of the same mind, thankfully, and without question, we help each other out of our suits as much as decently possible. My top is damp from this morning's surf, but In the van Jam hands me a blue hooded top, which I zip up gratefully, and pull the hood down over my eyes. The heating kicks in quickly, and we spend half an hour listening to Muse on the drive back to Newquay, Jam drumming away to Starlight on the steering wheel, laughing at my failed attempts to clap in time. My body is still freezing, though, and I just want to get into PJs and a robe, so I ask him to drop me off at the gallery for the car.

'Thanks for a lovely day, Jam.' I smile, stepping into the car.

Five minutes later I unlock Cain's door and sink against the wall in the hallway, wrapping my arms around the cotton warmth of the hooded top. I have the taste of the sea on my lips, but no regrets.

No bad ones anyway.

38
Jam

April

My flight leaves Newquay for London just after six thirty the following morning. I'm at Heathrow in plenty of time to catch my afternoon flight to Nashville.

I wander around a book store, looking for something to occupy my mind on the flight, but I can't find anything exciting. I pick up a few chocolate bars for Lucy, but I'm still not quite sure what to do with this excess energy or time. I don't even fancy a lunch time beer. Maybe I don't want to sit by myself?

I find a seat in the business lounge, fill up a plate of snacks and lie back with my headphones on, eyes closed, listening to the sound of the waves, until it's time for my flight. My senses are trying to tell me something, but I refuse to listen. I turn up the volume on the waves to drown out the niggles. I've never been nervous about flying before.

I'm glad I upgraded to a bed on the flight as I slept well, waking just as the stewards brought the evening meal around, half an hour before we land in Nashville.

I'd planned on taking a cab from the airport, but Cain is waiting for me at the arrivals gate.

'Hey, man, didn't expect to see you here!'

'Well, Lucy heard you were taking a cab and she dispatched me. She probably wants an hour or two away from me.'

'Unlikely, unlikely. But I'm glad she sent your ass out here, I hate waiting around. How's the album?'

'You've only been away a couple of days, bar a couple of listens, I've barely touched it. How was Elle's show?'

'Oh, so good, she has a natural way of expressing herself through her painting. Did you know she paints the ocean? She sold out while I was there, too, and after she believed me that I wasn't the buyer, we went celebrating in a pub.'

'Oh, you're killing me. There is something beautiful about a British pub. I miss them so much sometimes. Tiny, rowdy with the right music, gastronomic delights wafting past. Real. Ale. I really hope you had a few for me.'

'Well cider, yeah. And I see you trying to recreate a bar – sorry, pub – each time you have a party at home. Right down to lock in.'

For the rest of the journey, we talk about album and tour plans. When we arrive at theirs, I regale Lucy with Elle's show, and the British weather, and hand over the Cadbury's Dairy Milk haul from Heathrow. I had wanted to go back to mine, but the offer of a meal with family was too hard to turn down. Plus, maybe it'd stave off the quiet for a little longer.

I'd spent hours in the company of these guys, listened to their equal amounts gentle bickering and admiration for each other. But tonight, I did actually just need my own company. Maybe I hadn't slept as well as I thought on the flight over.

After clearing up the kitchen, I say good night. Lucy hugs me tight

'Thank you, again, for seeing Elle's first show.'

'Any time. Although it wouldn't also be her first show.' She digs me in the ribs and waves me off at the door. I love being with these guys, but I feel different around them, and I'm not sure why.

I close the door behind me, dropping my keys on an oak table. I'm stunned at the silence as I walk through a house I haven't really been in for weeks. The niggles return; something is off. But this time I just can't figure out what, even though I'm normally so tuned in to my senses.

It's probably nothing that a full night's sleep in a king-sized bed can't cure, I decide, climbing the stairs.

I wake naturally, just before dawn, felling okay. I go for a run on the trail, then shower and walk over to Cain's to work. I still feel like something isn't right, but it isn't enough to slow me down or block my concentration.

Bonnie and Patty are already in the studio, their arms resting on guitars, a coffee aroma in the room. Cain is making notes in his book, and all feels right in here. I sit behind my kit and begin working out an up-tempo song. Patty picks up the rhythm on her guitar, and Bonnie starts to hum a possible harmony. Unsure whether this is material for Cain or Bonnie, there is potential for further musical collaborations

We wind up work in the late afternoon and although there's always open house for dinner, I take a rain check.

At the store, I pick up some healthy groceries and at home I try to get out of my own headspace by stirring beef and vegetables around a pan. I don't want a lot of people around me, but I'm not sure I need to be on my own. I eat on my balcony, listening to the creatures in the forest.

For the next few weeks I repeated the pattern of working at Cain's every day, then heading home for dinner.

The silence became a little more familiar, and I liked the new routine of cooking and eating and sleeping.

Then one day in the studio he asks me if everything is okay, as I'm not around much lately. Had anything happened in England?

'Of course not.'

'Lucy misses you.'

I looked at him.

'Okay, maybe I do, too. A house full of girls, man.'

'You wouldn't have it any other way.'

'I absolutely wouldn't. Stay for dinner tonight, though, yeah? Lucy and I want to ask you something.'

'Ask away.'

'And give you the opportunity to skip out on dinner again?'

39
Elle

May

I grab my sketch book and pastels from my bag and hurry to the porch swing; that sunset won't hang around for long.

With surprising ease the pinks and oranges fly back and forth across the page, my thumbs bleeding the colours where they meet.

Hair falls across my eyes and I shove the annoying strands behind my ear. Using the black I sketch in the pine tree silhouette, only stopping as indigo heads towards midnight blue in front of me.

A long shadow covers the page.

The swing moves and my heart lurches. I turn around, looking straight up at Jam. A smile escapes from his lips and his hand strays out in front of him, eventually settling on the back of the chair.

'Good to see your pink back again, Elle.'

The break in my concentration flusters me. Then I look at my pink-chalked fingers and smile, shifting along the swing so that he can join me, if he wants to.

'Beautiful. You're so talented.'

'A camera would have captured the image just as well.'

He shakes his head. And I change the topic.

'Have you been here long?'

What was I saying? I should have just mentioned a couple of watermelons.

'I arrived last night'.

Lottie bowls into the garden then, and I place the sketch book beside me, running to scoop up my little chocolate monster. Jam brings my equipment inside.

The vast kitchen diner is a coordinated place of confusion to the untrained eye. Lucy and Cain serve plates and bowls of enough food until the table can barely be seen. I sit next to Lucy and Lottie, Cain sits next to Lucy and Jam.

'Can't believe we've eaten most of that', I declare a short while later, stretching back in my chair.

Lottie clambers up onto my lap and I twirl her hair between my fingers.

'Patrick is happy to make anything up in the retreat kitchen, just place your order before ten, as he nips out to the suppliers before lunch.' Lucy says, starting to clear the plates. Cain lays a hand on her shoulder, and takes the plates from her; Jam rises to help him clear the table. I pour more wine into her glass, and she sits back down.

'What else do we need to know about running the retreat this weekend?' I ask. 'I know you've emailed instructions for everything.'

Lucy nods. 'We only have four writers in, and Tallie is looking after them – you remember her; when she graduated in London, after some time studying in New England, she reached out to me for a reference, and I convinced her to start a PhD in American Literature with me. Well, she helps out at the retreat on weekends. It's more a case of you both being around to assist, in case anything happens.'

'And then we call you guys in Chicago and you sort it out, right?'

'Only if you never want to drum again.' Cain laughs, swatting Jam's arms.

'Never mind Jam, everything will run beautifully this week, as if you were still here. What do you guys have planned in the big city?'

'Oh, we're being proper tourists; we'll stroll on the beaches, walk along Navy Pier, maybe go on the Ferris wheel, take a boat across Lake Michigan. I can't wait.'

'Mummy says I can buy a new teddy, too.' Lottie whispers, in between thumb sucks.

'I bet it's the best teddy friend ever.' I giggle, my fingers stroking her face.

Jam makes coffee for everyone and Cain returns to the table, wrapping his arms around Lucy.

'And, as we're going to John Hughes' home town, I've booked us onto a special tour.'

'What?' Lucy exclaims, turning in her seat, while I soothe a startled Lottie.

'Mummy's just a bit movie-excited.' I laugh.

'We've had quite a busy year, I thought seeing places where Ferris Bueller and Sixteen Candles and Home Alone were filmed would be a great way to spend an afternoon.'

'Oh, Cain, that is perfect, and we'll have our gorgeous family with us.'

I haven't seen my sister so happy since she first moved to Nashville and they opened the writing retreat. But then I wasn't around nearly enough.

I take Lottie up to her bedroom, bathe her and help her brush her teeth, then we find her favourite Elsa nighty. We're just in the middle of a fairy tale when Lucy comes in.

I kiss my gorgeous niece goodnight and go in search of Em, who I'd heard wake up for milk a little while ago. I find her in her room, sat in Cain's arms as he holds the bottle to her hungry mouth.

I join him on the sofa.

'Good call on the movie tour.'

He smiles at me. 'I've been so caught up in the new album, I just wanted us all to have a few relaxed days together, before the tour starts. I don't see Lucy as much as I need to, so I want us to have a memorable trip.'

'Definite brownie points. You might even get to serenade her with some Simple Minds on the journey up.'

'Hey, not a bad idea, thanks.' He grins. 'So how are you doing in Cornwall? Is it too quiet for you?'

'It's just the kind of quiet I need. Your Mum is amazing and so creative. And I'm learning that I'm my own best resource – I don't necessarily need to please an employer.'

'Everything okay?' He asks.

I nod, not entirely sure where to start, so I don't bother.

'All good. I'm going on up to bed. Have a safe trip tomorrow.'

'Will do. You know we're always here for you? And this is your home, too.'

'Thank you, Cain.' I kiss his forehead, and then lean down to kiss Em.

Walking along the corridor to my room for the next few days I bump into Jam coming out of a bathroom.

'Good night, Jam.' I offer, continuing to walk away. He calls out my name and I turn back towards him. He seems like he has something to say, but just wishes me a good night too, thankfully.

That night I sleep fitfully, wondering how I'm going to be so close to Jam all week, when things are still uncomfortable between us.

The first couple of days aren't too bad. He spends a lot of time in the studio, and I look online for jobs I can apply for across Cornwall. My digital skills are strong; I just have to find someone willing to take a chance on me.

We eat dinner together in the kitchen, one or other of us retrieving the containers from Patrick before he serves the writers. I hardly see them, apart from on a morning walk around the woods.

It's on one of those walks that I spot the woman who brought Cain that basket last time I came to visit.

'Hey.' I call out. She sets off running into the forest. I run towards her and easily catch up with her.

'How come you're running?' I ask, blocking her way.
Her eyes dart everywhere.

'Remind me of your name again?'

I know she didn't tell me.

'Celene.'

'Celene. I'm Elle. Let's take a walk.'

My spidey-sense is very alert to something.

'So, how did you and Cain meet?' I start with. I may as well have just thumped her. I haven't. Not yet.

'We're friends.'

'It's good to have friends.' I confirm. Then, gently. 'But even better when that friendship is shared.'

She stops walking then, her eyes even bigger, if that's possible.

'These presents, Celene, they must be costing you a lot.' I remember the old looking books.

'Cain is worth it. His music makes me so happy.'

I smile at her now-massively-obvious crush. My spidey-sense is satisfied. I sit on a tree stump.

'He is a wonderful musician. He's also quite busy with his family.' My family.

'I know, I know. I come late at night, when it's quiet.'

'Do you live far?' I ask, picking up leaves, feeling their texture between my fingers.

'In the city.' She kicks at dirt with the toe of her cowgirl boot.

'Wow, it must be so noisy there. Do you live with your family?'

She shakes her head.

'I don't live with my family either. It can get lonely sometimes, can't it?'

She nods her head this time.

'What do you like to do? I like to paint.'

'I listen to Cain's music.'

Of course she does.

'Do you go to school?'

'No. I work in a coffee shop. No one talks to me there.'

'Oh, that can't be very nice?'

I look up at her, smiling.

'Do you think we could be friends?' I can almost see her brain processing this information. 'Cain's my brother-in-law.' I supply. 'Lucy, his wife, is my sister.'

She looks like she's about to flee.

'You're not in any trouble. I'll give you my email address, if you like, and we can keep in touch. I'm sure Cain would love to meet you, too. Properly.'

She sits down next to me.

'You have great taste in music. His songs really do speak to listeners, don't they?'

For the next fifteen minutes she talks non-stop about which of his songs she likes. I join in when she lets me. Then she asks me questions about life in England, and slowly it becomes a conversation instead of a diatribe about how brilliant my brother-in-law is.

We set off walking back and once we're at the house I spot Jam walking across from the retreat and call him over. I can feel Celene's tension already.

'Jam, I'd like you to meet a new friend I've met. This is Celene.'

He holds out his hand to shake and she freezes, then crashes into him. He looks so startled, but I hold back my laugh.

'Come on, Celene, let's go in and find some paper and I'll give you my email.'
She peels herself away from Jam, and follows me inside.

'Jam is lovely.' She says. Oh, no. Let's not.

'He is. So is his girlfriend.'

'Oh. I thought he was single.'

'They're keeping it secret. Can you keep the secret, too?'

She nods solemnly and takes the paper from me with my email address on. She agrees not to visit unannounced and instead of leaving presents, and wandering around the place, I suggest leaving a donation at the Veterans centre in Cain's name would be good. I walk her to her jeep and she hugs me goodbye. I hug her back. I know what it's like to have nothing and no one.

I wave her off and Jam joins me when she's safely off the drive.

'All sorted, Jam. But you have a secret girlfriend.'

'Sure I do. I don't even know about her.' He replies.

I make a mental note to ask Sarah to sort out some signed merch. I could raid the house myself, but I think Sarah needs to meet with her.

The following day, I make my way to the reception of the retreat, where Tallie is on the phone.

When she hangs up she smiles at me, waiting for me to say something.

'I'm happy to answer calls, and post messages on social media, if you'd like some time with your studies?'

She starts to say that isn't necessary and I give her that Ellie-Roar Rawcliffe look.

'Oh, well, if you're sure. I do have some research tasks I could work on.' She stands up from the stool and collects her bag from a shelf. 'Three of the guests are working in the shared dining room, and the fourth one, Karl, is out walking, looking for ... inspiration. I just hope he arrives back happier.'

'Well if he doesn't find it here....I'll let Patrick know. Hi, how was your walk, sir?' I ask a clearly sweaty man, presumably Karl. Tallie is busying herself with a nonsense task, her back firmly turned to him. I move my stool to try to disguise her shuddering shoulders.

'Simply awful. There are far too many bugs in the air for this time of year.'

'I am terribly sorry, sir, I'll be sure to pass your comments on to the management team. Perhaps a bottle of something at the table with your meal may help?'

'I would never turn down a Burgundy.'

'Consider it the pleasure of Nashville Narrators.' I stop just short of curtseying, lest Tallie rip apart from laughing.

He smirks then, as he retreats to the safety of upstairs and I watch him until he turns the corner.

'It's okay, you can laugh properly now.'

'Oh, I'm so sorry, that wasn't very professional of me', she titters.

'Oh, relax. You've seen how easy-going Lucy and Cain are – and I'm just as casual. Go on and enjoy your afternoon.'

I wave her goodbye and turn my attention to the computer, visiting the website and scrolling through social media posts. Bookings look good for the coming months. A few phone call enquiries come through and another two writers, who were possibly more engaged in each other than whatever notebooks they carried with them, wander past the desk for a pre-dinner stroll.

Is that what we're calling it these days, I thought.

'Well, well, well.'

I glance up at the voice.

'AJ?'

'The very one.'

I come out from behind the desk and hug him, grateful he doesn't try to kiss me, and especially not like last time.

'What are you doing here?'

'Would you believe me if I said writing?' he asks, his hands deep in his pockets. 'I honestly am! I've been trying to grapple with writing a Mark Twain biography, and I remembered your posts about this place. It is incredible.'

'Well, thank you. You're enjoying your stay?'

'Absolutely. The girl on the desk – Tallie?' I nod. 'She's been so helpful, finding trails for me to go running on, helping me locate texts. I gather she's a literature student?'

'Yep, my sister is her PhD supervisor.'

We chat for a few more minutes, and then hug again before he goes off for dinner.

The kitchen door swings open and Patrick hands me the dinner containers, of a beautiful roast dinner, just as I'm logging off. I head to the house.

'Hi honey, I'm home.' I call out, then swear softly under my breath when I realise what I've said.

Jam pokes his head out of the dining room, a bottle of wine in each hand. 'Red or white, dear?' He acknowledges, playing along.

'Everyone knows its white with chicken, lovely. Pop these onto plates while I freshen up.'

Jam mock curtseys and I draw my hands to my chest and nod in a Thai greeting, only aware I've danced across the line when his eyes seem to scorch into mine.

I sail up the stairs to my en-suite and hope I haven't buggered the evening up.

I spritz myself with the last few drops of my designer perfume, for a confidence boost, and head back down stairs.

Jam has set up places at the dining room table, seated opposite each other, the plates of chicken and potatoes still steaming and smelling delicious. I slide onto my seat, tucking a strand of hair behind my ear, and lick my lips. He raises his glass to me, and I join him.

'To a personal chef every day of the week.' He declares, lightening the mood.

'Absolutely.' We clink and fall into only a semi-awkward meal. The wine helps with relaxation.

'I need to talk to Lucy about offering Patrick a raise, lest he wander anywhere else.' I sigh, as I curl up on the sofa in the lounge.

'Too true, too true.' Jam paces, as if not knowing quite where to settle. He chooses a spot that is far enough away so that our limbs won't accidentally bump into each other, but we can still hold a conversation.

'Fancy watching a film?' I ask.

'Could do. Are you an eighties enthusiast, like Lucy?' I shake my head, sipping the wine.

'I need it to be twenty-first century at least, I'm afraid. Horror or comedy, though, I don't mind. You choose.'

He nods, fishing his phone out to stream a thriller to the TV. It wasn't hide-behind-a-cushion tense, but I jumped in a couple of places, causing Jam to jump, too.

When it ends he clicks off the phone and TV and announces he's going to bed, wishing me a hasty good night.

I remain on the sofa, in the semi-dark, drinking the remaining half-full glass of wine. Or, very likely, as half-empty, as I suddenly feel.

40

Jam

May

I slam the bedroom door shut and slide down onto the floor, trying to regain control over ... something.

I should have kept my distance from Elle, I shouldn't have set us up for an evening together by eating at the dining table. Should have just kept things light.

But dammit, she is so easy to be around.

Or not, actually.

Cain will need to install a drum kit in this room, so I have some way of distracting myself.

I stalk to the window, looking up at the night sky. Stars twinkle, and I slow my breathing down, almost seeing the disdainful look from Mom at my rude behaviour.

'I'll apologise in the morning.' I grumble and then start to close the curtains. A movement catches my eye. Elle, darting across to the writing retreat.

At this time of night?

I text her to see if she needs help, but there's no answer. Then I see her walking with one of the guests, their arms linked.

The next morning I skip breakfast, in favour of production work in the studio. By lunch I am starving.

Expecting Elle to still be at the retreat, I head to the kitchen for a sandwich.

I'm confronted with Elle, in crazy-sexy jeans, a beaming smile on her face, as she lays an amazing salad on the table, complete with a freshly cooked frittata.

'I only need a quick bite.'

To her credit she doesn't let any disapproval at my attitude show.

'That's fine; I'll put yours in the fridge for later.' Then she brings a fork to her mouth, her beautiful, full mouth, and makes the kind of sounds I don't need to hear right now. I stick my head in the fridge for leftover pasta and head back to the studio.

Two things interrupt my grumps: Cain does not allow food in the studio, and I've forgotten a fork.

A few hours later I have to come out, needing a beer. There is none in the fridge though. I pick up my keys and I'm heading out of the door when Elle appears from the lounge.

'Are you going to the store?'

I nod. Then I'm grumpier than Oscar the Grouch, when I realise her shirt has gaped open, revealing a black vest and heaven knows what lace beneath.

'Good. I need some things. You drive.'

A drive of ten minutes feels like eternity in purgatory. She hums to the radio, her hair blowing in the breeze from a rolled-down window. I shouldn't be able to smell coconut without the water nearby.

I turn into the parking lot and she hops out.

'See you back here in twenty minutes?'

'I only need beer.'

'Treat yourself.' She yells back, as I watch her retreating backside disappear into the crowd of cars and carts.

She is back at my truck, with two full bags of shopping, eighteen minutes later. Give her credit, she is a quick shopper.

I pop the trunk for her bags and she climbs onto the seat beside me.

Has she been trying on fragrances?

I glance at her as she clicks her seat belt into place, watching her studiously avoid my glare.

There is no humming or breeze this time, just the light tap-tapping of her fingernails on the door.

I lose myself into the beat and before long we pull up onto the drive.

Unclipping, she spins her head around to face me.

'You don't need to be so rude.' She admonishes.

'You were.'

'When?'

'When you left Thailand in the middle of the night.'

The fire that shoots from her beautiful green eyes stills me, as I realise a tornado is on the way. I am an arse.

'I had to.'

'It was rude.' And I was stupid, not knowing when to disembark the stupid train.

She starts yelling.

'You have no idea. Every time I saw you I wanted you in a way I'd never needed anyone. Any. One. You, this drummer in a bloody country band, parading around in vests exposing biceps that should be unnatural, were they not naturally developed from a devotion to the ocean, in cut-offs that revealed tan legs I just needed to wrap my legs around, long hair looking both unkempt and glossy like I wanted to grab and never let go, until your mouth found mine.'

I had not expected that response.

'I wanted you, too'. I whisper, pressing my lips to her startled mouth.

Just one minute. Let me just feel like I did when we were in this position in Thailand.

Responsive, why was she was so damn responsive?

I pull away this time and spring from the truck.

I have no idea where I'm going. I set off running towards the woods, not quite sure how to redeem myself until I've lost this energy I can't control.

41

Elle

May

I eat dinner alone that night, eating more out of necessity than enjoyment.

Jam returned from his temper some time ago, but he hasn't been near shared living spaces. Hasn't responded to my confession. Well, not verbally, anyway.

I spear the last of my asparagus and contemplatively chew on the green stalk. Slowly, deliberately, considering my next move.

There is only one.

I clear the table, washing and drying the dishes by hand, all the while trying to settle my mind.

Then I go upstairs, step into my shower and wash away the last few hours.

I pad, barefoot, slowly, towards my decision, wearing an oversized Foo Fighters' shirt.

Every common sense thought I've ever had yells at me to stop walking, but I'm helpless to instinct and I approach the door.

My hand quickly raps, imitating the pounding in the rest of my body. I eventually hear movement – good, I haven't anticipated that he'll be asleep.

He opens the door, a paperback in his hand. His navy blue vest looks new, damp, as if he's just showered. I hope my tongue hasn't just darted out like I suspect it just has.

'Three nights, Jam. Then I'm going back to the UK. Three. Nights. And one box to be emptied. Was that wanted, or want?' I launch the box I picked up from the store across the bed, gasping in absolute delight as his arm reaches out for my waist, dragging me to him and across the threshold.

The paperback thuds to the floor.

42

Jam

May

Elle. At my bedroom door.

 Three nights.

 'You're talking too much.' I declare, reaching out for her waist and pulling her into the room, ending up against the wall, drowning in her coconut scent. 'I don't know whether to torment the life out of you.' I draw my fingers, slowly and lightly, down her arms, her hips, watching her eyes deepen in their green. 'Or fuck you like I need to.'

 'Now who's talking too much?' She has a deliciously wicked grin. Then adds, 'Option B', just before her teeth sink into my shoulder. I lift her shirt over her head, just before my world goes black.

I'm awake, but I refuse to open my eyes.

 My hands connect with hands around my chest. Then I hear a little snore and slowly turn behind me.

 Elle.

 I smile as I open my eyes and face her. She sleeps like the dead and sounds like she's in the jungle. A content tiger.

 My content tiger.

 For the next three nights.

In the darkened room, I lean in and trace my tongue along her lower lip. She stops snoring, but doesn't open her eyes. My tongue continues its meanderings across her soft lips, my hands lightly tracing the curve of her waist and hips. She shifts ever so slightly towards me and whispers, 'Option A'. I nod and move her underneath me, rewarded by her beautiful smile. I have no time to wonder what we are doing. We're beyond that level of planning.

'Open your eyes, Elle.' She shakes her head quickly, although she's still beaming.

'Make me.' She demands, and I accept her challenge.

I can't hold out much longer, my body aches to be inside Elle.

I reach into the box and her legs part. For me. I turn back to her, her eyes open, staring holes through me.

'Please, Jam.' She whispers, and meets me as I move deep inside her, her mouth nuzzling my shoulder as we roar to satisfaction.

The next time I wake I don't need to see the sunrise to know she's gone.

I find her in the kitchen on the phone.

Her wet hair is piled onto her head and she's wearing a short, dainty, emerald sundress, which clings to her backside like I need to.

She blows me a kiss and I catch it like a teenager.

My stomach rumbles as she plates up bacon and pancakes. I set the table and bring the coffee. She rings off and dives right in to breakfast and plans for the day.

Hunger wins out over my need to talk and assess what had just happened.

I sweep up the food on my plate in record time.

She's still eating when I start to speak, but she shakes her head.

'Your place or mine tonight?' She asks when she's finished her mouthful. I grin and respond with her place, my heart flipping out all of its own accord.

She hadn't been kidding.

43

Elle

May

I hear the soft knock on my door a few moments after I've said goodnight.

When I pull back the door and see the disorientation in Jam's eyes I know answering naked has been the right choice.

He steps inside the room, lifts me into his arms, and carries me to the bed, matching each one of my bold moves with his own.

This time we stay awake as we settle into sleep, listening to the rain on the trees and the steadying of our hearts. As I drift asleep I hear him whisper, 'Just one more night' as he kisses my forehead. I pretend to be asleep.

And make sure I'm gone before he wakes.

I shower, wiling my muscles not to remember Jam too much, and dress in a pair of shorts and a band t-shirt. I walk to the retreat's office to relieve Tallie and work on social media for the Cornish guest house and my own website of sold-out paintings. I'd need more if my summer plans were to bear fruit.

I stick my head in the kitchen a short while later and Patrick rustles up sandwiches. I message Jam, hoping we'll have lunch on the patio together, but I don't hear anything from him all day.

Just before I lock up the reception, I receive a picture message from him. No text, just an image of the sunset I'd drawn on arrival day.

I close up and walk to the front porch swing, my erratic heartbeat matching my steps.

Jam stands next to the wooden swing, dressed in a suit, his hair tied back.

I stop walking and tilt my head in query. He outstretches his hand behind him and I tear my eyes away from Jam in a well-fitted suit, to see a table laid for dinner; candles blow gently in hurricane jars.

'Good evening, Elle,' he whispers, 'welcome to the House of Logan.'

He pulls back the silver domed cloches to reveal steaming plates of Chicken Pad Thai, quickly lowering the lids.

'I'll pour the – white - wine, if you'd like to freshen up?'

I nod and fly inside, straight for Lucy's room and her wardrobe; I know my fancies are all wrong, and she's been on several red carpets with Cain Adams.

Again, I smooth out the midnight blue jersey material, hoping my palms won't leave their mark on the fabric, as I walk, barefoot, on the grass towards Jam.

He stands and pulls out a chair for me, kissing my cheek and asking me how my day has been.

It takes me a moment to find my words, but this is the perfect end to our agreement.

I settle into the chair, placing a napkin on my lap to calm my nerves, and update him on my art plans.

He is an attentive listener.

After dinner, as the sun sets, Jam stands and holds out his hands for me. I stand; I can't not.

Soft sixties jazz begins to play and I snuggle into him, my cheek against his, his arms around my waist, as we slow dance around the porch. I literally could dance, dance, dance all night.

I'm not ready to go inside just yet. I sit on the porch swing, pulling him towards me, curling my body against him.

'I like this music, Jam.'

'Dad used to play it all the time. I spent hours looking through his vinyl records, hearing his stories about the artists and the musicians, which ones were Mom's favourite songs.

'Old-time soul in these songs. A time of innocence.' I feel him nod and he holds me closer to him.

'Neither Dad or Mom swam, though, that was Uncle Ed, out in Diego. He taught me to respect, not fear, the water.'

I tighten my grip around him.

'We spent hours in the ocean, body boarding, paddle boarding, surfing. I think he needed to do that to make sense of what happened.

'When I graduated school I brought the musical desire I had to Nashville. Not long later I bumped into Cain –

he was sure surprised to find an ocean-loving nut in a landlocked state. We headed to Maui after we walked out on a session. Seb and Sarah were off travelling in their van, but Cain and I needed the water.'

Whether it's the relaxed talk about a new side to a familiar story, or the connection I felt to Jam right now, I feel my eyes close. I'm helpless to fight my body.

When I wake, we're still in the same place, but Jam's jacket covers me and the sun is just making her appearance.

'I miss our sunrises, Jam.' I whisper, struggling to sit up, to lean closer to him.

'Me, too, darling.' He strokes my hair at my forehead.

'Where are WE at?'

'Who knows?'

'I need to go back to Newquay.'

'I know, sweetheart. Let's just be in this moment.'

I nod and in silence we watch the sun bathe us in light.

'Take me to my room, Jam.'

He lifts me easily from the swing and carries me to my bed. I cling onto him.

When I reawaken, Lottie is staring at me. I do a quick check behind me, but Jam has already left. I pull the duvet up and she squeals, throwing herself and a giant unicorn on top of the bed.

A smiling Lucy hurries in to fetch her daughter, apologising.

With memories of Jam lingering over my body, I shower and dress in jeans and a checked shirt and find everyone in the kitchen.

The trip has clearly been what Lucy needed. She bubbles with excitement recounting their week. I surreptitiously steal glances at Jam and he smiles at me, our secret.

We're good.

We *had* been very good. Or not, for three stunning nights.

But I was still flying out to the UK this afternoon.

He engineers it so that we sit together at the table, his leg casually resting against mine. I can barely talk for remembering how beautiful last night, and this morning, have been. I'm euphoric when he offers to drive me to the airport instead of Lucy. She's a little doubtful, not wanting to back down from a promise. But when she yawns, I suggest they all watch a film on the sofa, which I know is her Kryptonite.

In the truck, I sink into the leather seat, but Jam doesn't immediately start the engine.

I turn to him and he kisses me more tenderly than any man I've ever known. When he pulls away, he rests his forehead on mine.

'Elle, what I'm about to say, you don't have to say anything to. I love you. I have no idea beyond saying those words, and I don't-'

'I love you, too, James.' I blurt out, knowing I always have. 'I've had everything and nothing this year; *you* are all I need. Nothing else promised.'

He drags me to him, kisses me like I need him to.

I'm not sure which one of us pulls away first, we're both struggling to breathe. He smiles and reverses off the drive. I'm glad you can't get done for driving with the memory of a kiss.

I catch a glimpse of Lucy in the doorway, waving, her hand clutched to her mouth, as we leave the drive.

44
Jam

May

Elle walks nervously towards me for the first time since she'd issued her challenge, two nights ago, which I'd fallen headlong into.

The navy of her dress perfectly complements her eyes and I'm glad I'm holding onto the chair to steady myself.

As she approaches, her coconut scent refocusing my mind, I lean down to kiss her cheek.

I'm going to give her the perfect night of romance.

And then what?

I don't care if my heart will tear again; this night is just for Elle.

Elle stands before me, her arms loosely wrapped around my shoulders.   My hands are wrapped around her waist.

We're slow dancing to a jazz ballad, her steps perfectly mimicking mine.

In a few short hours she'll leave.

This is the start of our goodbye.

That night, as we bring the slow pace to her bedroom, I feel something inside me shift, connect and make perfect sense.

I stroke her face, neither of us speaking, as I watch her drift back to sleep. When she is safely in a deep sleep cycle I kiss her forehead and leave the room, knowing Lucy and Cain will return soon.

I'm just coming out of the shower when I hear their car pull up. I dress and go down to greet them. I hadn't thought they could look any happier, but there they are.

'Jam!' Lucy exclaims, pulling me in for a hug. 'Oh, thank you so much for staying. Was everything okay? Is Elle still sleeping? Did you have any problems? Oh, I'm talking too much, aren't I? We had the perfect trip, didn't we girls?'

Lottie tears off upstairs laughing, with a giant white unicorn under her arms.

Cain, having brought the last of the bags in hugs me and asks, in just the one sentence how things had been.

Offering the abridged version, I give, 'Just fine.' And make coffee while they unpack.

Lucy has brought Garrett's popcorn and Ghiradelli chocolates, for us, which she says Elle and I can fight over. I carefully put my mug down before I choke, managing to smile my thanks.

Elle comes downstairs a few minutes later, Lottie chattering away to her.

Everything around me quietens as I just focus on Elle, the way her clothes hide every curve I've spent three days tasting. Her tired, yet searching, green eyes land on me, a soft smile on her lips as she tucks a strand of hair behind her left ear.

There must have been conversation, as I see people moving and laughing, but it was like I was in my own sound booth, Bose earphones on.

As plates are gathered, my non-visual senses tune in and I realise breakfast is on the way. I situate chairs and mugs, so that Elle's coffee is right by my right hand side. Then Lucy, with her keen attention to detail, the girls and then Cain.

In twenty years from now I couldn't tell you what I've eaten, but I know that Elle's legs never leave mine and six times our arms manage to touch inconspicuously.

I know Lucy has offered to give Elle a lift to the airport.

'Thank you for a gorgeous brunch, Lucy.'

'Oh, he speaks.' Cain laughs. You must have been exhausted from looking after this place, you've barely said a sentence that didn't start with pass the...'

'When food tastes this good a man would be a fool to talk too much.'

'Excellent save, Jam. Besides, I was talking enough for everybody.'

'I also imagine you'll be quite tired from the hectic trip. I don't mind driving Elle to the airport.' She was more miserable at that suggestion than I'd anticipated.

'That's a great idea, Jam.' Elle steps in. 'Why don't you guys relax with a film? I'm sure the girls would snooze on the sofa with you?'

Oh, there was no way Lucy was resisting an offer like that.

'We'll all see each other again in Cornwall, when you come to visit in a couple of months. You have UK dates planned, don't you, Cain?'

'Yes, Mum and Dad have reserved the guest house for us all in July, and we're playing a few weeks across the UK, starting with the West Country, for the album launch.'

'So, us girls will have loads of time to catch up then.' Elle finishes, hugging her sister, then returns upstairs to pack.

I try really hard to remain in my seat, in case I sit too long in the truck waiting for her. Within half an hour she is down, a large canvas in her hands, which she offers to Lucy, of the sun setting over the Lizard headland.

More hugs later than I realised two women can give, we were in my truck.

No matter what happens in the next minute, I had something I needed to share, with the only woman I've ever truly cared about.

She responds to my goodbye kiss as I need her to. Then the words I never hoped to hear, 'I love you, too, James,' she'd replied. 'I've had everything and nothing this year; all I need is you. Nothing else promised.'

No one on earth knows me better than this woman.

And she loves me, too.

I kiss her again, knowing it won't be the last time we'll be together, but just in case it is.

When I reverse the truck off the drive, I catch Lucy smiling and waving us away. Has she been crying?

45

Elle

May

This time when I board the plane to the UK, away from Jam, I'm not in pieces.

Being an adult sometimes hurts, but the fissures will heal.

Besides, I have work to do.

Another gallery in Newquay has contacted me about showing, next month, and I only have a handful of paintings I'm happy with.

I'm glad both Lucy and Cain loved their new piece of the Cornish headland overlooking the ocean. I'd only ever known city skylines, but it was the water I'd paint forever.

During the flight I watch a couple of comedy films, eat half a meal and manage a few hours of sleep before our descent. My eyes smart from exhaustion and I hope to continue my sleep on the connecting flight to Newquay.

I feel the memories of Jam on every part of my body, on every minute of the nine hour flight back to the UK.

Mostly bloody good memories, tinged with sadness over the distance. But I need to understand more about my own plans before I can plan to be with someone else.

As the plane touches down at Heathrow, and I make my way to catch my connecting flight, I'm already thinking about the work I have ahead of me.

I have to.

The taxi drops me at Cain's house just after four.

There is around an hour left before sunset. I throw my luggage inside, gather my pad and coloured pencils and lock up. I follow the coastal path to Little Fistral and sit on the sand to capture my first sunset after knowing that I love Jam. The vibrant pinks and purples don't do justice to my feelings, but I know exactly where I'm placing this and I didn't think Jam will mind.

I return to Cain's for the car, put the canvas on the passenger seat and drive the short distance to my favourite place in Cornwall.

Unlocking the door to Jam's house, I take the stairs two at a time, to the top floor. I place the A4 canvas in the middle of Jam's bed and share the image with him, with the caption, 'First Love. Where's the beach?'

He replies instantly with the correct answer and sends me a photo of his forearm, with the caption, 'Missing my First Love.'

I remove the painting and climb into Jam's bed, my sticky face sinking gratefully into his pillows.

46

Jam

June

After I'd dropped Elle at the airport, gained a parking fine and almost caused her to miss her flight, I'd returned to the car in a bit of a daze, Elle's body imprinted on mine, her coconut scent filling my truck.

I drive back to my house via the grocery store, clean through the house and try to watch movies to distract myself from missing her so damn much. I must have fallen asleep, because I wake, disoriented and cold. It's pitch-black outside. My body clock is obviously in sympathy with Elle.

I'm half-heartedly toying with a chicken dish I've made for a late dinner when my phone pings, to tell me I've received an email.

I grin when I see it's from Elle, and then push my plate away when I open the attachment of her painting. On my bed.

And the caption.

I know how the oceans and tides feel. And I feel like I'm swimming against the tide.

Only six more weeks until I can watch the sun sink on Little Fistral with her.

I reply to her message then share a picture of my arm, wishing it was wrapped around her.

Is this how Cain feels all the time?

Oh, shit. How am I going to tell Lucy about my love for Elle?

The following afternoon I ask Lucy and Cain if I can use their kitchen to cook them a thank you meal, for all the food they've provided for me. Lucy doesn't hesitate in throwing me the oven gloves and they spend the hour playing with Lottie and Em; I can hear the squeals from their garden as I prepare the fried fish and chop the potatoes ready for frying.

After the Nashville Fish and Chip supper, complete with malt vinegar and Cornish sea salt, I bring out the dessert of homemade sultana scones and strawberry preserve. I don't miss their exchanged look.

'What's on your mind, Jam?' Lucy asks.

'You two have always treated me as one of your family.' I reply, knowing these are the wrong people to play games with at any time.

Cain wraps his arm around Lucy's chair. I don't miss that exchanged look either.

I take a deep breath, trying to find the right words.

'Elle is the elusive Mrs Jam, right?' Lucy suddenly says.

'What, now?' I pretend to mishear, folding my hands into my lap. Watching their faces I realise they're about to explode with laughter. How long have they known?

Lucy sits up then, reaching for my hand.

'I am so happy for both of you, Jam. Honestly.'

'What?' I am so confused. 'When?'

'I came out to ask if everything was okay, on Elle's last morning. I noticed you hadn't set off. Then I realised why.' She clutches her heart, leans into Cain.

'Do you love Elle?' Cain asks.

'Like you love Lucy.' As soon as I say the words I know they're true.

We might not have promised each other anything, but where the hell did this leave us?

Back at home that night I wander through the house, rearranging items on shelves, examining my space through new thoughts. How long have I been in love with Elle? Probably since I'd hauled her out of the waves at Kynance Cove, when I realised first that I could have lost her before I'd gotten the chance to know her. I'd been so shook up that afternoon. Maybe that's when I'd begun to see Lucy's kid sister from another perspective?

Maybe last August, when I'd turned down her offer of sharing a bed.

And then immediately flown to San Diego so that I hadn't done anything stupid, like knock on her door.

In Thailand I'd tried to share my love for her, as I'd watched the city-dweller disappear so that an ocean-loving woman could emerge, who had just known me.

And reached out for me.

Like she had done only last week, throwing us both off-course.

I hadn't expected that she would love me in return, or that my body would miss hers so much.

I sit behind my kit and record a video for Elle, feeling heavier and lighter all at the same time. How long until I can see her again?

The next few weeks are taken up with the hectic onslaught of Nashville hosting hundreds of thousands of eager country fans, for the annual CMA Fest. It has grown immensely since its origins as Fan Fair in 1972, for five thousand fans, and there are shows to see as well as deliver, from early morning through to early morning all along Broadway and her surrounding streets.

We had several performances before headlining at the Nissan football stadium on the Friday night of the festival and we had three other appearances across the long weekend. But there was a host of interviews lined up for Cain, and Seb and I made the most of turning up randomly in bars and at other sessions, to watch the expressions on people's faces and to have a good time. I provided percussion support for Bonnie and Patty at their slots, watched as word spread about their talent. Cain brought them out to one of his shows on the riverfront stage and the country crowd roared their approval. I got to jam with some of country's greatest musicians, too.

I should at least stop thinking about Elle all day long. Shouldn't I?

Not at all, it turns out.

I wanted to share everything with her this time, show her why Nashville is so amazing. Introduce her to so many people who I know she'd warm too.

I sent so many photos of different events, and shot glasses, that she probably couldn't make sense of anything in 2D.

Which is when I solicited Lucy's help in setting up a special surprise.

47
Elle

June

I'd quickly adapted to the time difference, learning that Nashville was six hours behind the UK, as most messages from Jam came through in the afternoon and evening.

I'd gone from working throughout the day, to painting in the evening and using the late night to catch up on social media. I'm still at Cain's, although spend a lot of time in Jam's garden.

It was from his garden one evening that I rang Lucy. After polite family talk she came right out and told me she was so happy for me and Jam, had sensed an interest for years. I watch the sun set over the Atlantic and we had the best sister talk we've had in years. There are so many missed moments between us, because I worked all hours in Boston, instead of spending time with my family. I can't wait to see her again next month.

Tim and Jake have asked me to manage their digital marketing campaigns, helping to build their audience engagement. One of the commercial properties they invested in was Fion's gallery. He cleared off to Mexico, with a comfortable financial incentive, and they sourced a British art director to manage the gallery's artists and their work. My Cornish paintings have permanent residence.

Zed is still shopping up a storm in Boston, for the stationery company, travelling frequently between China and the US. I've asked him if he could package up my remaining belongings and I'll collect them next time I'm in the US, although I've told him I'm not returning to live on the east coast. I have no idea where I'll live, now I have the freedom of and desire to travel. I can work anywhere. I wonder if this is how Cassie feels, planning which countries she could visit next. The choice is vast and I love the potential.

I sleep most of the day now, and from daft o'clock until silly o'clock every dark o'clock, I manage the PR of my growing list of US clients and catch up with Jam.

But I'm still surprised when I receive a message from him as I'm eating breakfast, one morning, before heading to speak with a gallery owner in St Ives, thanks to a helping hand from Mo.

I open the video attachment, burrow into the sofa and reach for my coffee.

Sat at his drum kit, a white Led Zep vest displaying bronzed arms, he smiles at the camera before counting down into the opening of a familiar track. The Foo Fighters' most romantic song, Everlong.

From the moment he sings Hello I place my cup carefully down, in case it shatters from my hands.

I am lost, and so, so found.

When the song finishes he looks up and smiles at me.

'Good morning, Elle, just wanted to let you know I'm thinking of you. No promises, just lots of love from Nashville to Newquay.'

I lose track of how many times I replay the video.

The giddiness subsides, paving the way for inspiration. I've never drawn a self-portrait before, but I grab my nearest pad and sketch out my side profile in pencil, using the very first art techniques I learned. I put the backdrop of the ocean behind me and a big, shaded heart for Nashville on a map I'm staring at. Then share it with Jam.

Thankfully, I'm not late for my meeting.

The following week the notifications on my phone go crazy. I've signed up to the CMA Fest app, as I know Cain is playing several dates across the weekend. I troll my social media feeds for footage of the band, although predictably most shots are of Cain and Seb at the front of the stage.

I send Jam some photos of my new collection, featuring abstract images of the sunset, blush pinks and pale purple horizons. Then another video comes through on his account. I check the timings and I know this is their headline slot.

I hit the triangle in the centre of my phone and I'm immediately treated to Jam, liquid behind his drums, on the main stage of what looks like a huge football stadium. But the camera is only trained on him. His energy, and those arms, which in three weeks I'll have wrapped around me. A few times he smiles for me, and the videographer.

At the end of the quickest three minutes, Lucy turns the camera on herself, with a massive thumbs up.

Each act only has a thirty minute slot during the main shows at CMA Fest. I wait half an hour and ring Lucy. She picks up straight away, squealing.

'I can't believe you and Jam! He's so good! He's so sweet!'

'So you're really okay with the news, then?

'Absolutely, yes, and I still can't believe you're the elusive Mrs Jam.'

I roll my eyes and after another few minutes catching up I ring off. I go to bed, Lucy goes to a party.

48
Jam

It has been seven weeks since I've last seen Elle in person, and as I follow Lucy and Cain's van, on the drive from Newquay's airport to The Lizard guest house, I know it's the last hour I ever want to be apart from her. I have no idea how we'll work, but I know that we will; our messages and conversations since May have decided that.

A radio station plays nostalgic hits and as the opening notes of Randy Travis' Forever and Ever, Amen play, the volume instantly goes up. I watch Lucy and Cain continue towards their destination and I indicate right to turn towards mine. I park the rental car, staring out at the cloudless blue sky for a moment, an expanse of ocean below. Then I step out to stand at the edge of the cliff, the turquoise water in Kynance Cove quiet and still.

My shoulders feel lighter in the presence of the water, as always, and then a streak of colour darts from the beach into the ocean.

Elle's pink is back.

I take off running down the sheer drop, my feet easily handling the pebbles below me. Arms out for balance I pick up speed as I skip over the natural step formations.

I strip off my t-shirt and jeans, as I cross the small beach to the shore, flinging the material on a nearby rock. Striding in to the water I spot the pink easily and swim towards my future.

49
Elle

July

I sense movement alongside me and spin around.

Damn tourists not knowing their range. I've checked and the beach is empty.

Then, familiar muscles stretch out of the water, followed by those deep chocolate eyes I've done nothing but dream about all summer.

'Your hair!' I exclaim, as all six foot two of Jam treads water in front of me, his new cropped hair highlighting his sexiness.

'That was going to be my line.' He laughs, tucking a strand of my pink hair behind my ears and kissing me hard. Like he'd been thinking about doing all summer, too.

I'm in danger of drowning from my aches at his proximity. I wrap my body around him, letting him know how much I want him. I nod slightly, smiling and he understands, his eyes widening before nodding in agreement.

I would always love unnerving this man.

He glances around quickly, but I already know the beach is deserted; we wouldn't need long.

'There are five major oceans in the world, Elle.' He rasps afterwards. 'And I want to see the sun sink into each one of them with you. Then we'll start on the seas.'

'Let's not forget the lakes' I grin, a different kind of ache in my body now, as I play with Jam's new hair, twirling the curls at the back of his neck.

'And rivers.' He adds.

'I bet there are some cracking reservoirs out there.' I love challenging him.

'Streams.' He answers; he is the only man whose challenges I need.

'Just imagine the reflection in a puddle.' I stretch the theme.

'Just imagine creating art and music together across the world.' He finishes.

'Just what I was thinking.' I pull him towards me, vowing never to let go of everything, ever again.

Epilogue

Elle and Jam

September

I look out of the airplane window, the southern Californian coast line now far below me, the last four weeks of family and surfing and diving blurring away into so many shades of blue.

The man next to me leans over to catch a glimpse of the view, no doubt checking out the surf. His arms wrap around my shoulders.

I lean back into Jam, his warm breath tickling my neck.

'I've had the best month.' I sigh. 'Eddie and Mel are so lucky to live here.'

'Say the words, Elle, and we'll move into the San Diego house that Eddie has no doubt set aside for us. He's smitten with you.'

'Smitten?! You have such an old-time soul, Jam.' He trails kisses down the back of my neck and I'm so in love with him, body and soul. 'Their beach wedding was just perfect.'

'We don't have to stay in Belize, we can hop onto the next return flight. Well, maybe take advantage of the hotel for a day and night, or two. As long as I'm with you, Elle, we can be anywhere. Cassie won't mind if we don't meet her in Ecuador.'

My sighs threaten to increase in volume, at what Jam is doing to me and the thought of literally being anywhere in the world with him.

'We could stay, but it would be a shame not to see Belize's Barrier Reef, or explore her many islands.'

I had cuddled the travel bug this last few months; the band had spent July touring the UK, from their base in Cornwall, and I'd loved spending time with Lucy and the girls, disappearing into tucked-away, rocky coves. Lottie is taking after her Dad with her love of the sea so we ate most meals on the beach.

I'd been to every show, all across the UK, watching Jam from the wings and dragging him off stage as soon as I could.

In August we'd all flown out to LA for west coast shows, driving along California as the extended family we are. Tallie and AJ had joined us for the Burning Man music and art experience in Nevada, and seemed pretty excited to be wandering off into the desert together.

Last week had been the pinnacle though, celebrating the marriage of Jam's Uncle Eddie to Mel in San Diego. I definitely left a piece of my heart on that shoreline.

'Besides', I add, pulling his arms tighter around me, 'the touring must have taken its toll on you this summer – you could be in need of a rest.'

'Hmmm, rest.' He murmurs; we both know we have no time for that. Now I'm PADI accredited, we'll be living under the water for the next month, before joining Cassie at her school in Quito. Jam will teach drumming, and I'll teach art classes, until we return to Thailand in December.

A steward approaches with a trolley and we settle back in our seats for refreshments.

'What are we drinking to?' Jam asks.

'Cain developing the careers of other musicians in Nashville so we can travel?'

He nods and we clink our glasses.

'To Cassie inviting us to South America.'

'To Cassie.' I confirm. 'And visiting the equator. And the gazillion other adventures we'll have together.'

'Together.' Jam nods, putting our glasses on a nearby trolley, turning me in his gorgeous arms as his lips seek out mine.

Wonder how many hours are left on this flight?

Acknowledgements

Oodles of grammatical gratitude to my editor, Liz Taplin, who ~~endured~~ enjoyed lots of rewrites with me to polish the syntax of the story; extra Jorders points for making sense of the four AM emails, Liz!

To Pete and Eve, who kept themselves entertained every weekend when I was buried in the craft room, crafting the details of the *Everything* series, growing the characters and ~~losing~~ weeding the plot; extra Jorders points to Pete for not minding (too much) when I crept into bed as the sun rose. Extra Jorders points to Eve for developing her own narrative skills through copious amounts of telly watching.

Thank you to all my family and friends who have read along and celebrated every step of the way with me. Especially those who read outside their usual genre.

Massive social media shout outs to all of my fabulous dgtl readers (especially Gillian Docherty and Cecyl Garin!!) who read and reviewed the story of Lucy and Cain in **Everything, Except You**; those reviews, and your generous shares are always wonderful to read. Extra Jorders points for anyone who fell for Cain.

This series is for every romance reader out there who also believes that love is everything.

Reviews of <u>Everything, Except You</u>
Book 1 in the Love is Everything series

*****

Loved the characters and the storyline had me hooked!
Not just for country music lovers but did enjoy the story
around our UK country star. A MUST read and was also a
great surprise the next chapter is still to come and can't
actually wait. Perfect gift
GD, Amazon, November 2019

*****

Well, I just finished reading 'Everything, Except You' written by
Emma Jordan and all of my 'loves' were fulfilled. I was
fascinated to get to know the characters - Cain and Lucy came
from different worlds and common sense told me they were
unsuited, but as their relationship grew, I found myself willing
them on. The story is set against a background of Cornwall,
London and the United States and the author's clever
contrasting and comparing of these places added value to the
story outline. The unusual and the fast-moving structure of the
story kept me turning the page and I was constantly saying to
myself 'just one more chapter'.
LT, Amazon, January 2020

*****

Really enjoyed the flow of this contemporary romance
story, the characters are developed well and the storyline
was engaging.
Already looking forward to book 2
HLB, Amazon, February 2020

*****

Loved this book! Really enjoyed following Cain and Lucy on their journey, especially with all the country music references. Lots of yummy food references too! A very enjoyable romantic light read. Looking forward to the next two!
J, Amazon, February 2020

****

This was an easygoing read to dip in and out of. The characters were great, they're relationship developing - bringing the best out in one another.
JP, Amazon, April 2020

*****

Everything, Except You by Emma Jordan is a modern day Gift of the Magi. What would you do for love? What would you give up? This couple's journey is 'everything' you want in a romance novel...
"I'll be eating irony and drinking misery!" Jordan has a way with phraseology, it's fun, it's witty, it's a little snarky and makes the pages of this book fly. The main characters are people you want to know and root for. Oh, and the obstacles they face — you'll be anxious!

This debut romance will have you following this author clamoring for the next in the series. Trust me.
M, Goodreads, June 2020

Coming soon...

Everything at Christmas
Winter 2020

Everything for Her
Summer 2021

(Yeah, the characters have had a word with me and decided that they have many more than the original three stories planned).

Printed in Great Britain
by Amazon